Finding

Mercari

By

Shaquana Jackson

Printed in the United States of America

First Printing, 2021

ISBN

Sophisticated Real-Life Publications

P.O. Box 988

Abbeville, La 70511

www.shaquanajackson.co

The sharp slap across the young girl's cheek echoes like a thunderclap. Her knotted hair swings as her head shoots to the side, the black-gloved hand retreating into the darkness. Her brown eyes are wide as the sting burns on her cheek.

She's so thin you can see her ribcage through her soft brown skin covered in weeks' worth of filth. She's wearing only a torn shirt and panties that used to be white but are now stained gray with muck and grime.

Hot tears mix with the dirt on her face as she shifts away from her attacker on the hard, concrete floor. A heavy rope is double-knotted around her wrists and ankles. This isn't the first time someone has hurt her. Purple bruises and crusting scabs are littered up and down her skin, ugly blotches of injuries from weeks of abuse.

"Look at me. *Look at me!*" shouts a tall white man. In the murky half-darkness, he looms above her like a monster. He has a black beard straggled with gray, dark hair slicked back. He gets on one knee in front of her, cupping her aching chin to turn her to face him. "You see what you make me do?" His voice is quiet now, making goosebumps stipple across her skin.

His fingers, calloused and dirt-stained, run down her neck to her chest, which rises and falls in fear at his touch. He pauses at her bare thigh, leaning in to run his foul tongue over her cheek and down to her neck, the whiskers of his beard scratching her skin.

She cringes away from him, a dry sob escaping her throat. "Please," she cries, her skin crawling. "Please don't do this."

"You caused this," he says, grabbing a fistful of her hair and yanking her head back, making her wince.

"Please," she whispers, tears dribbling down the sides of her face. She can smell the horrid stench of alcohol on him, the filth and piss of her prison. Terror overwhelms her. He likes it when she begs, but she can't help it. "I'll do whatever you want. Please, just let me go home."

He pulls away, leaving a damp trail on her neck. "We gave you plenty of chances to act right," he says, almost whispering, his hot breath rank on her burning cheek. "But you never listen, do you? And now no one wants to buy you."

He chuckles in the darkness, showing several white teeth. "You're putting a damper on my business. You were supposed to be sold a long time ago, but you keep giving me trouble, Pebbles. Just look at your face," he grasps her chin and turns her face side to side. "And your body," he gestures to the old cuts and bruises on her shoulders and legs.

He roughly pats her jaw before getting to his feet.

"If you let me go, I promise I won't tell anyone about you," she whispers, though it's no use.

The man's laugh echoes around her prison. As his body shakes, the meager light from the dusty old lightbulb above catches in a blade sticking halfway out of his pocket.

"Doll, please, you forget who you're speaking to," he chuckles, a humorless sound that sends chills down the girl's young spine. "You know my face. Why in the world would I let you go? You'd run straight to your parents, and what'll they do? Tell the police. You'd be a superstar, trending all over your little town in no time. Then this nice little operation I've got going here would be shut down."

The girl whimpers, edging against the dirty stone wall.

"I might as well walk into a police station and fall on my knees saying, 'take me now!'" He waves his hands in the air, laughing at his joke.

His cell phone buzzes in his pocket, a piercing electronic sound that's startlingly real compared to this hellscape.

"This must be instructions on what to do with you," he says smugly. He winks at her, approaching a wooden cabinet as he brings his phone to his ear.

"Can I use the restroom?" she asks.

He glances at her in disgust. "Just use it where you are. You're already filthy."

Several cabinets are scattered around the room, some with weakened or missing doors. Dry stains are all over the concrete floor, some a shade of dark brown that the girl suspects is blood. Her blood, maybe. Her cheek still stings from the slap, and she's gotten more cuts and bruises these last few weeks than she can count.

She just wants to go home. Her normal teenage life of high school and her family feels like a distant dream, another lifetime.

The man is muttering into his phone with his back turned to her.

"Can I please use the restroom?" she asks, her voice stronger.

"Alright, man, I got it," he says to the phone, ignoring her plea. "I'll get rid of her."

He hangs up, turning to stare down at her. He comes over in two quick strides and yanks her to her feet by the elbow. She cries with pain as he roughly turns her around and slices at the rope around her wrists. He cuts it away from her ankles, too, and the dirty rope falls away, leaving blistered skin in its wake.

The girl sees her chance and takes it. As hard as she can, she kicks the guy in the shin, and with a rough gasp and a stroke of luck, he drops the knife with a clatter. Grunting in shock and pain, he stumbles back, grabbing his leg. The girl darts towards the knife when his cold fingers wrap around her ankle. She screams as she crashes to the floor. Wincing, teeth gritted, she reaches for the knife, but it's too far for her to reach, and her fingers scrabble against the concrete.

"Stupid… kid!" the guy roars, pulling her back. She kicks out, landing a kick on his nose, which gives a satisfying crack as his grip loosens. She scrambles over to the blade, her hand closing around the hilt, and jumps to her feet, pointing it shakily at him. Terror screams through her mind, heart pounding.

Holding his nose, the man's voice is muffled as he lets out a strange chuckle. "You're crazier than I thought," he says. "You know you've messed up, don't you?" He gets to his feet as the girl leaps back, the knife trembling before her.

"Now, let's not be silly," he says, holding up his hands. Blood is gushing out of his nose, staining his lips and beard. "Give me the knife, and I won't make this any worse for you."

"No!" she screams. Tears are burning her eyes as terror pounds through her veins. "I'm going back to my family!"

"You don't want to do this. Listen to me," he says, taking a step towards her.

"Get back!" she cries, swinging the knife in a wild arc.

"I can make this as painless or painful as I like," he says. "I'm the king of torture. The longer you do this, the longer it'll take for you to die. I'll make sure of it."

"Stop!" she screams, tears sliding down her cheeks as he takes another step toward her. "Get away from me!"

The knife gleams in the weak light, trembling in her dirty fingers. There's a sudden noise outside, and her attention moves to the door for a fraction of a moment…

It's all he needs. Her attacker darts towards her, tackling her painfully to the ground. Agony shoots up her back as his heavy body pins her down. His hands grab clumsily at her waist and her arms, trying to grab the knife. Pain throbs in her ribs as his foul breath spills putrid over her face, fingers scrambling for the blade. She struggles, hugging the hilt close as he tugs. He shoves her over, him on top, growling through his teeth to give him the knife…

His fingers slip. The blade drives down into her stomach.

Her body goes frigid. Pain bleeds through her abdomen as they both look down to where the blade is buried in her belly. Blood, hot and red, gushes from her skin, pooling on the ground.

The man gets to his feet, watching as the girl's breath slows, her eyes wide with terror and pain as her mouth hangs open in a silent scream.

"Stupid kid," he says finally, sighing like this is a mild inconvenience. "Should've just given me the knife. I'll send a note to your parents, don't worry."

He wipes his arm across his face, grimacing at the nosebleed. Leaving the girl bleeding out on the floor, he strides to the door and opens it. The night is beyond, a strong wind howling in the trees and blowing in icy air. There are no stars, but the pale glow of a crescent moon hangs in the sky.

The girl's body stills, her final breath leaving her, staring sightlessly at the grubby ceiling. Shaking his head, the man throws her still-warm body over his shoulder, smoking a cigarette with his free hand. Exhaling gray smoke, he steps out towards where a hastily dug hole is waiting. He lowers her in, staring down at her filth-covered body, the look of horror frozen on her young face. There's no mercy in his heart for his victim, no compassion or stroke of regret. Only disappointment that he didn't get to torture the defiant little cow first.

Taking another deep inhalation of his cigarette, he grabs a shovel and piles the dirt on top of her. No ceremony. No words for the lost life.

He throws away his cigarette, stamping out the glowing ember with his boot.

#

The morning dawns bright with white puffy clouds in the air. In the town of Grandville, twenty-three miles away from the shallow grave, Jasmine is late for work.

Her hair a mess and her face bare of makeup, she hurries into the town news office, a briefcase in one hand and a stack of papers tucked under her free arm. She tugs at her black skirt, red heels clacking on the floor. The newsroom is full of people walking around, calling instructions to each other. At the far end is the brightly lit desk, one of Grandville's reporters getting her makeup redone before the next live news report.

Jasmine takes a left, where glass double doors lead her to an office room with people at computers, typing up reports or discussing in low voices. Microphones and cameras are on the desks, ready for use. A coffee machine stands in the corner, a godsend for many of the hardworking souls here. The myriad of noise – the tapping of keyboards, low voices, the sizzling crack of the coffee machine – makes Jasmine wince, but she's used to it by now.

She stops and opens her briefcase to get the rest of the papers inside, not looking where she's going, and she collides with someone. With a gasp, the papers slip from her fingers, and they make a terrific mess on the carpeted floor.

"Oh, gosh," Jasmine moans, getting to her knees to snatch up the papers. "I'm so sorry. It's my fault."

A dark-haired man kneels in front of her, helping. His hair is neatly combed, and when he looks up to smile at her with several papers in his hand, she's met with dark eyebrows and warm brown eyes. He's wearing a black suit with a yellow tie. It's Taylor, the Italian American producer for Channel 5.

"Not to worry about it."

She exhales, taking the papers and stuffing them into her briefcase. He smiles at her with perfect white teeth.

"You okay?" he laughs, waving a large hand. She blinks.

"Sorry, yes. Just got a lot going on," she gives a nervous laugh, gesturing to the mess.

"It's quite alright," he helps her to her feet after they've checked for stray papers. "If…"

"Uh…"

They speak at the same time and grin shyly at each other. Nearby, Shelby glances at the pair over her glasses perched on her long nose. She's Jasmine's coworker, a Caucasian woman wearing a gray pencil skirt, dark hair tied in a bun, and bright red lipstick just within the realm of professional.

"Listen, I have something you might want to check out after we grab coffees," he says.

"I'm all in," Jasmine smiles.

"Hey, Jas," says Shelby, winding neatly through the sea of bodies to approach her. "I see you made it in this morning," she holds a manilla folder against the chest, smiling to show her comment isn't malicious.

"Yeah, barely," says Jasmine weakly.

"Understandable," says the older woman, her piercing eyes glancing at Jasmine's frazzled curls. "You overwork a lot. Better take care of yourself; this job can get overwhelming at times."

"I will, Shelby. Thanks."

Shelby gives Taylor an odd look before striding off. Raising their eyebrows at each other, they get some much-needed coffee before Jasmine follows Taylor to his desk. It's overcrowded with papers, loose bits of stationery, and a little bobblehead of a happy-looking dog. He slides his coffee cup onto a patch of desk stained with brown circles and types on his computer. Jasmine watches, sipping her latte from her mug, *Bossup* written on it in cursive.

"You see, there's a pattern that might tell us who's taking these girls," says Taylor, getting up a report of the missing teenagers that have disappeared in the past several months. He links his fingers behind his head, leaning back so Jasmine can peer at the screen.

"I don't understand."

"We've managed to track these girls to the same app, Teen Space. It allows the suspect to connect with these girls and groom them. Then they meet up with him, and..." he sighs. "Murders them."

"Wait," Jasmine removes the cup from her lips, nausea churning in her guts. "Murder? We haven't put any information about girls being murdered. Just missing."

Several people nearby fall silent as Taylor glances up at her.

"Jasmine, you can't be that naïve," he says quietly. "You really think, with all this time that's passed, the girls are still alive?"

He sits up in his chair.

"Excuse me," she says weakly, the coffee cup shaking in her hands. "I'm not feeling well."

"Jas!"

She doesn't look back as she dashes out of the newsroom, her lungs suddenly tight. The pictures of the girls, all between twelve and fifteen years old, flash over and over in her mind like strobe lighting.

Murdered...

#

Taylor sighs, glancing over at Jasmine's desk. She's left the briefcase on top of it, her coffee cup beside it. On her desk is a framed photo of a pretty little girl with a shock of black curls and dimples in her cheeks.

#

Jasmine still isn't feeling well. She left work early today, taking a breather at home. Now she is at the kitchen table, scattered with newspaper clippings and posters of the snatched girls from the last several months. *MISSING* dominates the headlines, and each photo of a girl is like a needle pricking Jasmine's heart.

"Okay," she mutters, tapping her chin. She's researched the app that Taylor mentioned. Teen Space is some sort of new chat room where you're randomly matched with someone based on your interests and hobbies. Of course, the growing concern about it has just heightened its popularity. "What do these girls have in common for you to choose them?" she mutters to herself. She isn't a detective, but the word "murder" has sent alarm bells through her mind. Grandville isn't that big, and the number of girls that have turned up missing this year alone is alarming. Aren't the police doing anything?

"Mom?"

Jasmine gasps, her heart jumping. She was so engrossed in her research that she didn't hear her daughter's approaching footsteps. "Mercari," she gasps, "You scared me."

"Sorry," Mercari giggles. She wraps her arms around her mother's waist, her thick, wooly hair tickling Jasmine's shoulder. She's wearing her blue jeans and dressy pink shirt with matching flats.

"Mom," she says in a small voice. She's using that innocent tone she uses when she wants something. "May I have a cell phone?"

Jasmine pulls back, sighing. "Cari, we've been over this time and time again," she says. "My answer hasn't changed." Her eyes dart to the pictures of the girls. For one horrifying moment, she sees Mercari's face plastered on one of those news headlines, bold letters spelling *MISSING*. Her shoulders tense. "You're only thirteen; you don't need a phone yet."

"Really, Mom," Mercari's eyes roll. "Everyone at school has one. I'm the only one who doesn't –"

"Stop exaggerating," her mom cuts her off. "You take everything to the extreme. Not everyone has a phone, Cari. There are a lot of parents who feel the same as I do. When I was a kid, we didn't have phones, and we were fine."

She cups Mercari's chin, kissing her cheek as her daughter pouts. "Let me get you some orange juice."

"No, you're right. Only the cool people have phones," Mercari says sulkily. "For God's sake, I'm a teen already."

Jasmine slams the orange juice on the counter, annoyance rippling through her. The way her daughter's behaving, you'd think she was deliberately torturing her.

"Cari, come here," she says, snatching up the nearest paper from the table. "You see this girl?"

Mercari swallows as her mother flaps the paper in her face. She knows the girl; she's a grade above her. She's been missing for two months.

"She's missing because of a phone." She snatches another paper off the table. "This girl, too. And this one. All because of the same reason: a stupid app!"

"Okay, okay, Mom," says Mercari, raising her hands. "I get the point."

Jasmine breathes hard through her nose, rearranging the papers as the doorbell rings.

"I'll get that," says her daughter, looking all too happy to escape the tension in the kitchen.

"Mercari…"

"I'll just get the door. Who is it?" she calls. There's no answer.

Mercari pulls open the front door, showing their neatly trimmed lawn facing a suburban street. No one's there. She steps outside, looking around, a light breeze tickling her hair. She doesn't notice the man watching from around the corner.

Jasmine's blood runs cold as there's an ear-piercing shriek from outside. She dashes past the table, knocking several papers to the ground. "Mercari!" she yells, running for the open door. "Mercari!"

Her daughter doesn't respond. She bursts outside and clutches her chest, relief exhaling from her. Mercari's in her father's arms, giggling as he tickles her mercilessly.

"Oh, God," Jasmine breathes, sagging against the wall.

"Dad, stop!" Mercari giggles. "I can't breathe!"

Shaking her head as her heartbeat slows gently,

Jasmine composes herself, folding her arms as she watches. Her husband… well, estranged husband, Kel, wraps his large arms around their daughter and pulls her into a cheerful hug.

"My friends might see, and I'd lose a lot of cool points," says Mercari, giving her dad a playful push.

"Yeah, I bet," Kel chuckles, patting her head. He looks up and sees Jasmine. "Hey."

She doesn't say a word, a mixture of annoyance and relief flooding through her. Her fingers are still trembling. Kel's face falls, and he says comically, "What did I do now? I just got here."

"You scared me half to death, that's what," says Jasmine, feeling suddenly cold. She rubs her arms.

"Yeah, Mom's been a little paranoid lately," says Mercari.

Sensing Jasmine's about to spit fireworks, Kel quickly says, "Well, that's understandable, sweetie. Don't some of those missing girls go to your school?"

Mercari and Kel follow Jasmine inside. "Can I get you anything?" she offers.

"Coffee would be great, Jas, thanks." He glances around at

the kitchen tiles.

"Yeah, sorry about the mess," says Jasmine quickly. In her panic, she knocked most of the loose papers to the floor, and the floor's covered in several dozen newspaper clippings and "missing" posters. "Honey, could you pick those papers up and take them to the living room for me?"

"Sure thing, Mom," Mercari gives her dad another quick hug and picks up the papers as Jasmine works the coffee machine. "I'll be back."

"Here," she offers the coffee to Kel.

He takes an appreciative gulp and asks, "How've you been?"

"Pretty busy, as you might be able to tell," she sighs. "Since those poor girls came up missing, you know," she gestures at the table. They both take a seat. Jasmine nervously taps her fingernails on the wood, a crease of worry between her eyebrows.

"I actually wanted to talk to you about Cari," says Kel in a low voice. "She mentioned she wants a cell phone.

Well, I agree with her. She's already thirteen…."

Jasmine hears a creak of floorboards outside the kitchen. It's too quiet in there; Mercari's probably listening.

"Listen," Kel says as Jasmine opens her mouth to respond. He gently places his warm hand over hers. "I know how you feel about cell phones. I was the same. But she might need it one day. She can use it to keep in touch with us."

Jasmine slid her hand out from beneath Kel's, ignoring the warmth he left on her skin. "I'm not about to get into another argument about this," she says, getting to her feet with the scrape of a chair.

"That's your problem," says Kel, leaning back and crossing his arms over his chest. "Everything must go your way, or else. I'm her parent too, remember? You only think about your feelings." He stands, too. "If you would listen for once –"

"Go ahead, say it!" Jasmine says, her voice raised. Kel can be so damn annoying sometimes. The stress from work and her worry is building up into a ball of rage. She isn't in the mood to deal with him right now. "Why our marriage is like it is, huh?" She wants to throttle him. Instead, she slams the wood with her fist. Pain shoots up her knuckles as they glare at each other.

"My gosh, you guys, you can't be left alone for one minute without screaming at each other," Mercari snaps from the doorway. "You're both so selfish. Don't you know how it makes me feel?" Dark hair bouncing, she turns tail and stomps off, leaving them both staring at each other.

#

The next day is windy, fall leaves blowing on the concrete. A young girl dressed in a gray and burgundy plaid skirt and a white button shirt walks home from school, her book bag on her back, bobbing her head to the music from her earphones. She walks under a tree, branches overhead, drying red leaves swirling around her ankles. Her blonde hair, tied in a braid, bobs as she hums to herself along with the music.

Behind her, a red car approaches. Dried mud is splashed across the tires and the bottom, staining it to an almost opaque brown. A man with a black, graying beard licks his lips as his window lowers.

"Hey, excuse me," he calls out to her. This close, over the

purr of the engine, he can hear the muffled blast of music. She looks

so young, so fresh. He drives closer to the sidewalk until his car is

moving level with her pace.

The girl glances at him, pulling out her earphones as she

gives him a wary look. Her breathing quickens as she looks around,

glancing ahead as though tempted to run.

The man sputters. "Hey, hon, I'm really sorry to bother you,

but I was wondering if you knew where the nearest pizza joint is?"

he squints to the road ahead, a suburban block with a neat row of

houses.

The girl's gaze travels over his long hair and piercing blue

eyes. She doesn't respond.

"I heard there's one somewhere around here, but I swear I've

driven up and down these streets for an hour. I just want some dang

pizza, ya know?" he gives a hearty chuckle, rubbing his beard. "I'm

kind of new to the area."

She finally clears her throat and says shyly, "Uh, yeah.

There's one just around the corner. Your second left." She points ahead, avoiding his gaze.

"Oh great, I appreciate it," he grins at her. "Well, you have an amazing day, sweetie." He waves at her.

The girl doesn't respond, lowering her head as she puts an earphone back into her ears, walking along at a quicker pace than before.

"Hey, listen," he stops the car, and she turns around. "If you like, I'll buy you some pizza. A small thank-you for helping me out." He winks.

"No, thank you," she mumbles, turning tail and speeding off.

The man's smile disappears as he watches her go, eyeing her skirt and pale legs. He kills the engine and gets out of the car, pulling on the black cap he keeps on the passenger's seat. He takes a white cloth from his pocket and has a look around. The street is quiet, a little early for the usual time to come out of school, and the scene is clear of other cars, neighbors, or pets. His long legs moving him forward, the man approaches the girl. About thirty feet away, she's slowed back down, sticking the other earphone in her ear as the tension in her shoulders loosens a little.

He raises the rag in his hand, then fear floods him when a man in his sixties suddenly appears, jogging from his garage two houses away. He lowers his hand, sticking the rag into his jacket pocket as he whistles.

The older man runs on the other side of the road but stops when they're level, watching him. He points at him, and they stare at each other. Sweat springs across the bearded man's forehead as he hastily adjusts his jacket.

"Hey, man!" the jogger shouts, pointing at the ground behind him as he pushes his glasses up his nose. "You dropped something."

He looks around, but there's nothing there — frustration ripples through him. The girl is getting away.

"No, behind you."

That's when he spots it – his pocketknife, sitting on the curb near the road. He snatches it up, clearing his throat. He nods at the jogger, and the man smiles, sticking his earphones back into his ears and jogging away.

He takes another deep breath, sighing as he watches the jogger until he turns a corner. Turning the pocketknife over in his fingers, he strides after the girl. His tall frame reaches her easily, and he taps her on the shoulder.

She jumps a mile, her eyes widening as she whirls around, ripping the earphones out of her ears. "What do you want?" she stammers.

He raises his eyebrows, pulling the rag out of his pocket. The terror in her blue eyes only makes this moment sweeter. "You!"

#

"You know, I'm fine walking home on my own," says Mercari, checking her watch. It's a bright pink thing her father bought for her eleventh birthday. A little childish, but she's never quite had the heart to throw it away.

"I don't mind waiting with you," says her teacher, Ms. Meadows, smiling down at her. "This is actually part of my job, so you'll be doing me a favor if you stay. Mothers know best, right?" She tucks a blonde curl behind her ear.

Mercari mutters something unintelligible, glancing towards the road. Everyone else left twenty minutes ago.

Meanwhile, a frustrated Jasmine beeps her horn. There's a smoky old blue car in front of her, somehow going ten miles an hour and simultaneously blocking the entire road. Probably an elderly person.

"Dammit, does it make sense to drive so slow? Like, damn," she mutters, slapping the steering wheel in her frustration. "Some people have got places to be, buddy."

She finally bypasses the car and is hit with a red light, forcing her to stop. She growls through her teeth, leaning back in her seat. She doesn't dare check the time; she knows she's already late.

#

"Hi, Mr. Johnson, it's Sheila. Mercari's teacher," says Ms. Meadows. "I'm at your daughter's school, and she's the only student here again. It seems her mother is a little late picking her up."

Ms. Meadows glances over at where Mercari's getting a drink from the vending machine.

She hears an impatient exhalation over the phone. "Alright. Thank you. I just happen to be around the block, so I'll be there in a second."

"There's no need to thank me, Mr. Johnson," says Ms. Meadows, subconsciously playing with her necklace. She smiles, biting her lip, then turns and comes face to face with Mercari, who's watching with a raised eyebrow.

She's saved from the awkward silence by the approaching hum of a car engine less than five minutes later as a black BMW rolls into the driveway in front of the school's reception area where they're waiting.

"Daddy!" Mercari cries in delight, running to meet her father. Ms. Meadows watches her go and throw her arms around Kel. *What a lovely father. Mercari's crazy about him.* The scene makes her smile.

"My baby girl," he says fondly. "Did you have a good day?"

He looks up to Ms. Meadows. "Thanks again for staying with her, Miss…?"

"Sheila," she responds, sticking out her hand.

"Sheila," Kel repeats. Exchanging warm looks, his dark eyes meet her hazel ones, and they shake hands.

"Dad, can we go now?" asks Mercari, heading to the car. "I'm starving."

"Have a great afternoon, you two," says Sheila, unable to resist twirling a blonde hair in her fingers. She knows Kel and his wife have separated, so he's fair game as far as she's concerned.

"Yeah, you too," Kel smiles back, dimples deepening in his cheeks and making Ms. Meadows' heart flutter.

Kel's driving when he gets a call from Jasmine. "No worries, Jas, I've got her," he says into the hands-free.

"I'm sorry, guys. I got held up at work –"

"Yeah, Jas," Kel glances at Mercari, who's sitting with her lips pursed. "The same excuses."

The phone crackles as Jasmine sighs. "Well, if you haven't noticed, we have missing girls to report on! It's my duty to bring awareness to it, Kelvin."

"That may be so, but you can't keep leaving our daughter

hanging like that," he says as they turn left onto a busy street. "You have to learn some responsibility, and that includes putting our child first. Do you want her to be next?"

There's silence on the line.

"I'm upset about the girls, too," he adds in a softer tone. "But we have a daughter who needs us."

"Daddy," says Mercari, looking up at him.

"Yeah, baby?"

"Please… stop with the back and forth," she says, her voice quiet. "It's driving me crazy."

Hearing her on the end, Jasmine's voice rings through the car. "I don't have time for a lecture, Kel. I know my responsibilities just fine. I can meet you and pick her up. Where are you?"

"It's Friday. I'll keep her with me, Jas," he says. "Work on getting your issues together, okay? Figure out what's important to you."

"Kel –"

"This isn't up for discussion!"

"At least let me talk to her."

"She's on handsfree. Go ahead."

There's a short silence as Mercari bites her lip. Then she says in a voice that breaks Kel's heart, "You forgot me again, Mom."

"I'd never forget you, honey. I was late," says Jasmine. "Listen, I'll make it up to you, I promise."

"Yeah, Mom. Of course," Mercari sounds tired like this isn't the first time she's heard her mother say this.

"I love you, Mercari. From the bottom of my heart. Mommy will make this up to you, okay, sweetie?"

"I love you too, Mom."

Mercari sighs through her nose, leaning back in the seat and watching the trees and buildings flit by.

"Kel, thank you again," says Jasmine. "No matter what situation we face, you're always there. I'm serious. We really appreciate you."

"Yeah, Jas," says Kel, concentrating on driving and only half-believing what his wife's saying. "I'll call you when I'm on my way to bring her home."

#

Jasmine hangs up the phone, worry drumming through her. She's only five seconds away from the school, damn it! Another couple of minutes, and she'd have been there. It isn't her fault Shelby had piled a bunch of extra work on her twenty minutes before it was time to leave. Facts had to be checked, stories written, the privacy of the missing girls' families respected…

A black Mercedes passes her car, and Jasmine recognizes Mercari's teacher, Ms. Meadows, who gives a friendly wave as their cars pass. Jasmine gives an awkward nod and smile in return, reversing away from the school grounds.

#

Mercari's mood lifts when Kel pulls into the yard of a two-story yellow house. Her eyes widen in delight. "Grandma's place!" she fumbles with her seatbelt, missing the clicker twice in her excitement. "I haven't seen her in ages! I've missed her."

As Kel locks up the car, the door opens, and Mercari's grandmother stands on the threshold wearing a beautiful blue sundress, her wrinkled face smiling as she opens her arms for Mercari to leap into.

"I've missed you, my child," says Martha, kissing Mercari's forehead.

"Missed you too, Grandma."

"Come inside. I just baked a fresh batch of chocolate chip cookies. I know how much you love them."

"You know me so well!" Mercari dashes inside with glee as Kel grins behind her. "Hey, Ma."

"Hey, baby," Martha coos, kissing her son on his cheek. "You're looking a little skinny there yourself, son. You eating right?"

When they venture inside the well-lit home decorated with framed photos of the family, many of them Mercari when she was younger, they find her in the kitchen, a half-eaten cookie already in her hand.

"How are the cookies, baby?"

"Grandma, nobody can bake cookies like you," says Mercari. "No matter how old I get, even when I'm seventy, I'll still love them."

Kel and Martha chuckle as Martha puts on the kettle.

"That's my baby right there," Kel laughs, patting his daughter's dark curls. "She'll be staying with us for the weekend, Ma, that alright?"

"Her mother didn't give you a hard time, did she?" Martha asks, raising an eyebrow.

"She was late again to pick her up, so I thought I'd bring her here." He swallows the biting remark, *"Where she'll be monitored."*

Martha's hand reaches her hip, looking at him like she can hear the malicious thought in his mind. "Huh. Figures." She rolls her eyes as Kel rummages in the refrigerator for some orange juice. "Sweetie, you could do so much better than her. Messing around with a woman like that…."

"Momma, please," he says, his cheeks tinging with

heat. "She's still your granddaughter's mother, and though we're separated, she's still my wife. I still love her," he adds quietly. "And she'll always be Mercari's mom."

"That's okay," Mercari calls, getting to her feet. "I'm used to Grandma bashing my mom."

"Of course not, sweetie. I would never bash your mother," says Martha, preparing Mercari a glass of milk.

"Sure, Grandma," Mercari doesn't bother to hide her sarcasm. "May I be excused? I just lost my appetite."

"I'm not surprised, scoffing all those cookies," says her dad, but he looks worried.

"Of course, baby," says Martha, her dark eyebrows knitting with worry. "I didn't mean it like that. Oh, by the way," she puts the milk on the kitchen counter. "There's a gift for you on the bed. I was going to bring it to you, but there's no time like the present." Her face breaks out in a smile as Mercari looks up at her with innocent eyes. "Oh, sweetie, you're just so beautiful. Come give Grandma another hug."

Mercari doesn't smile back as she wraps her arms around her

grandma, inhaling her powdery old lady scent.

"I'm so glad you're here, love bug," Martha mumbles into Mercari's hair, gently rubbing her back.

"I'll meet you upstairs in a minute," says Kel.

"Okay, Daddy," she gives her father the peace sign.

"Momma," he rounds on his mother as soon as Mercari is out of earshot. "You shouldn't say things like that in front of Cari."

"Say what?" asks Martha innocently, wiping away crumbs and straightening the tablecloth.

"Disrespecting the mother of my daughter," he whispers. "Who, by the way, is still my wife."

"Oh boy, don't remind me," says Martha, her eyes rolling to the ceiling.

"You're going to end up losing your granddaughter if you keep talking like that, Ma. And I know you don't want that."

Martha nods, laying a hand on her chest. She's wearing a pale blue ring that matches her sundress. She's a burst of color, always favoring bright clothes and hair accessories, even in winter. "You're right," she sighs. "Even the thought of losing that precious child is too much to bear." Her dark eyes go glassy.

"Love you, Ma," says Kel, planting a kiss on her forehead. He jogs upstairs and taps on Mercari's door.

"Come in."

He goes into her room, where Mercari sits cross-legged on the bed, a new notebook in her hand and surrounded by wrapping paper. Martha has a three-bedroom house and uses one room for her granddaughter, the other for storage. There are still many childish things about the room: a chest of drawers full of old toys, puzzles on the shelves, a shelf of old children's books gathering dust. Kel stands at the threshold, smiling at his daughter.

"What, Dad? Is there something on my face?" she giggles.

"You look so much like your mother." He sits on the bed beside her. "Listen, I'm sorry for what Grandma said –"

"It's okay, Dad."

Kel takes his daughter's warm hand in his. "No, it's not

okay. I really am sorry." He tucks a stray curly hair behind her ear with a smile. "I know you've been through a lot lately, but I just want you to know that no matter what your mom and I go through, we both love you dearly."

Mercari lowers her head.

"Do you hear me?" he said gently, guiding her face back up until her eyes meet his.

"Dad," she says softly. "I don't want you and Mommy to get divorced."

Her words make his heart hurt like there are shards of glass in his chest. Her lip trembles.

"I love you both so much, and I thought you loved each other, too," she gives a rattling sigh. "But you're gonna get a divorce, right?"

She swings her legs off the bed, looking so miserable that it makes Kel want to tear up. He swallows the lump in his throat and says, "We'll talk about it later, okay? Properly. Take it easy for now. I know you've had a busy day."

#

Nerves tickle Jasmine's belly as she descends the stairs. Her hair is gathered in a neat bun, and she's wearing a red dress, matching heels, and crimson lipstick. As her heel hits the last step, a flash of lightning illuminates the whole house, making her groan.

"Ugh, you've got to be kidding."

Rain pounds on the windows, a thundering crack in the sky following the lightning rumbling in the sky. She didn't even know it was going to rain tonight. She stares at the foul weather in dismay and jumps as she hears a sudden bang at her front door. Did she leave it open, or…?

"Taylor?" she calls, her voice shaking. "Is that you?"

She opens the front door, looking out to where heavy rain lashes the street before her. The wind howls somewhere, and she gasps as the cold wind whips at her dress. Rubbing her arms, she glances around as she hears another banging noise, this time from the garage. It sends a jolt of fear up her spine.

"Taylor, is that you?" she shouts into the rain-filled night. She steps out into the storm, instantly drenched with ice-cold rain, making her gasp. The door slams shut behind her. "No! Damn it!"

Her teeth chatter as she grabs the doorknob. It's jammed. She yanks at it, cursing through her teeth. If she's been locked out…

She jumps almost out of her freezing skin when someone taps her shoulder. She screams, whipping around, but it's only Taylor, holding an umbrella, concern on his handsome face.

"You okay, Jasmine?"

"Oh God, Taylor, you scared me!"

He glances at the door behind her, to her rain-soaked dress and hair. "Is everything alright?"

Now her heart rate is slowing, and Taylor's here for their date. Jasmine feels foolish. She laughs, suddenly aware of how terrible her makeup must look. Another growl of thunder rumbles in the distance, and she has to shout for him to hear her. "This might sound crazy, but I can't get my door open. Damn thing's jammed. Typical, huh?"

Taylor turns the knob and gives it a slight push, opening it.

"Thanks," relief mixes with shame, heating her cheeks as they step inside. Water drips onto the carpet as Taylor folds his umbrella. "I'm sorry about that. Let me get you a towel."

"I think you need one more than I do," he says gently, gesturing at her sodden dress and hair. She grins at him.

"You're right. I'll be right back."

After drying off and redoing her makeup, Jasmine feels much better. It'll be the storm making all that noise outside. She overreacted.

"I brought you some flowers," says Taylor as she heads back downstairs. He's wearing a fancy-dress suit and pants, looking like a million dollars. "They're a little dripped on, but…."

"Aw, thank you," she says, taking the lilies. "They're… well," they both giggle nervously as the flowers droop. "They're still beautiful."

Ten minutes later, the duo is eating salad and baked fish by candlelight, a loaf of crusty bread between them.

"Where's your little one tonight?" asks Taylor. The flickering candlelight reflects off his dark hair and olive skin, and he eats with a grace that makes her heart flutter. The storm still rages outside, rain lashing on the windows and the occasional flash of lightning illuminating the room. Safe and warm and eating by candlelight, it feels cozy. "I hope she doesn't feel like she has to stay out of the way?"

"Well, no," she sighs, a ripple of anger running through her at the way Kel spoke to her today. "She's with her father." She clears her throat and takes a sip of red wine.

"You say that like it's a bad thing," he remarks, noticing her tone.

She half-smiles, swirling the crimson liquid around in her wine glass. "No, not a bad thing," she says, taking another quiet sip. There's silence in the kitchen, the thunder and lashing of rain the only sound between them as Taylor takes another bite of salad.

"It can't be all bad," he says finally, nodding at the wedding band still glittering on her finger. "You're still wearing that."

Flushing, she covers her hand instinctively. "Well,

the separation is still fresh," she admits. "Kel has his flaws, but in many ways, I still love him."

The smiles vanish from Taylor's face as he puts down his fork.

"I'm sorry," she said quickly. "I didn't mean it like that. I mean…" she sighs. "I'm so confused."

"It's alright," he says, wiping his mouth with a napkin, his smile returning. "I understand this is all new."

"You're so sweet and understanding," she says, her right hand reaching across the tablecloth. A ripple of heat flows through her as his dark eyes meet hers. The candlelight reflects in his eyes as he leans in and plants a soft kiss on her lips.

Warmth rushes through her. It's been a long time since someone kissed her like this. She opens to him eagerly, her arms sliding around his shoulders as he cups her face in his warm hand.

Excitement threads through Jasmine, and for the first time this evening, she's glad Mercari isn't here to walk in on them. The rain patters on the roof, enclosing them in a safe, warm space, all alone…

Taylor's hand slides down her neck to her breast, making her gasp in delight. Then her phone suddenly rings, a stark and piercing sound that yanks her back to reality. She groans into his lips and reluctantly pulls away.

"I'm sorry, I've got to take this."

She gets up from the table, staring outside as she speaks into the phone. She can't see anything except her reflection in the glass, and her lipstick smudged from the kiss that still burns her mouth.

"Oh God," she says into the phone. "Yes, yes, of course. I'm on my way."

They exchange a look and quickly pull on their jackets.

"I can drive," he offers.

"Don't be silly. How would that look?" she snaps.

"I don't think you're in any state to drive. How much wine have you had?" he says as they step out into the rain. He holds his umbrella above them both as Jasmine opens the garage. Taylor's car is parked on the street nearby. The rain has lessened, now a gentle patter and the storm has ended, leaving a cold breeze in its wake.

"I'll meet you there," she says shortly, climbing into her car. Wiping away the lipstick in her rear-view mirror, she glances down at her dress. The jacket will have to keep it covered. When she's called to report on a crime scene, there's often very little time to prepare. She hoped she wouldn't be called tonight.

Her heart sinking, Jasmine backs out of the garage, windscreen wipers sliding across the glass as she follows Taylor's car towards the address Shelby gave her. It isn't far, and she can see the blue flash of police car lights long before she parks behind Taylor on the street.

It's a beautiful place, a neat neighborhood, the kind where nothing bad ever happens. Cops are standing all around, and a woman with blonde hair wearing a long gown is crying into her husband's chest, clutching a photograph as a cop stands before she holds a pen and notepad, poorly disguised pain on his face. Sadness and fear churn in Jasmine's guts as she flags down Shelby.

More cops are knocking on neighbors' doors, flashlights

piercing the falling rain. A damp wind tickles Jasmine's hair as she takes a breath, trying to turn her nerves to professionalism.

"Hey," says a soft voice. Taylor is behind her, his eyes sad as he scans the scene before them. "This feels like… it almost doesn't feel real," he murmurs. "Why does this keep happening to all those sweet babies?"

Not for the first time, thoughts of Mercari flitter across Jasmine's mind as she looks at the mother, the parent of the latest victim. To say she's heartbroken would be an understatement. A shattered woman stands before her.

In moments, Shelby and the others have thrust a microphone into Jasmine's hand, an umbrella in the other. A readymade screen telling her what to say is ready as a cameraman approaches a middle-aged, serious guy named Sean she's worked with before.

"No time to waste," says the brisk voice of a fifty-year-old white woman, the rain landing on her beanie hat as she fusses around Jasmine's hair, straightening her jacket collar. Taylor gets behind the camera, giving her the OK sign and then counting down. "Three, two, one…."

"Welcome to Channel Five News," says Jasmine, pulling on her professional mask. "We have some breaking news here tonight. Another child has gone missing in our town of Grandville." Her hands shake slightly. "Lisa Brown is only fifteen… fifteen years old."

Her lip quivers as she reads from the screen, the grimacing faces of her coworkers silently urging her on.

"She didn't return home from school today. This is the seventh child that has gone missing… gone…" her voice cracks as emotion overwhelms her, bubbling across the surface. Her eyes fill with tears as people watch in silence.

She's never had an emotional moment on live television before, but the rush and the shock of another missing girl are threatening to overwhelm her.

Taylor's large hand waves at her, his eyebrows raising. She clears her throat, her shoulders relaxing. When she speaks again, her voice is clear. "This is the seventh child that has gone missing in the past four months. She was last seen wearing a white shirt and a plaid skirt. She's described at around five foot two, with long blonde hair usually worn in a braid. If you have any information regarding Lisa Brown, please contact the local police. The number is at the bottom of your screen."

The cameraman signals that the connection is cut, and Jasmine lowers the microphone, sighing as a wave of emotion crashes over her.

"You alright?" asks Taylor, rubbing her shoulders as Sean and the others pull away. He flinches from Jasmine like he's burned her when a gray-haired woman approaches. She's a senior editor, holding an umbrella over her head as she points at Jasmine with her free hand. "I know you're distraught about this, but when you're reporting the news to a live audience, you must keep it together," she scolds. "This is your job, and it has to be done right. Hundreds, perhaps thousands, just watched you lose your cool on air."

"I know," says Jasmine, deflating. The rush of emotion has left her exhausted. "I'm sorry. I just feel so angry and hurt that someone is snatching these poor girls, right under our noses, and we haven't found any of them that might be alive…" her eyes prickle, and she blinks away the threat of tears. "Oh God, Taylor, I have a daughter! What if she…?"

She doesn't want to say it aloud, but it screams like alarm bells in her mind. *What if Mercari is next?*

This is a nice neighborhood, the kind of place where families live. The kind of street where people have barbecues and go to church and are in bed by nine o'clock. And a girl was snatched off the street. No one in Grandville is safe.

The gray-haired woman shakes her head, clacking away on heels that don't much help her short frame. Jasmine breaks down, and Taylor's warm arm wraps around her shoulders.

"Shh," he soothes, pulling her close. His warm fingers caress her head, leaving tingling warmth on her hair. "I know, I know. I hope they catch this bastard."

#

There is barely any light on this barren country highway, twenty miles away from Grandville. A rusty black truck, conspicuous on a crowded city street but not out of place on this dark, quiet road, rumbles along with the dirt, the only lights from the headlights illuminating the path before it.

The driver bobs his head to an old tune on the radio, the glow of a cigarette between his teeth. He turns onto an old driveway with a crunch of gravel, approaching a lonely two-story house surrounded by overgrown plants and grass, old tire rims, and toolboxes. He pulls up and kills the engine, sighing as fatigue prickles his eyelids.

His black boots land on the ground outside, throwing dust into the air. The storm of earlier has died away, leaving the scent of wet pine needles in its wake. He throws down his cigarette and crushes it beneath his boot, looking around. Without the truck's lights, there's not much to see. Trees rustle in the wind, the moon obscured by thick clouds. His heavy footsteps take him to the back of the truck, where the faintest sound comes from within. He opens the trunk, and there lies a little blonde girl, tape around her mouth and her wrists and ankles tied together, sniffling. There are dried tracks of tears on her cheeks, her blonde curls a tangled mess.

Her eyes widen as he watches her, a silent scream in her gaze. Gray tape covers her mouth. He grins down at her, a rush of heat tingling in his groin at the sight of the girl so prostate and helpless. The last one was too rebellious. This one's fresh.

Insects chirp in the darkness, twigs and leaves blowing across the dirt as the man gathers the girl roughly in his arms. She sobs, wriggling feebly in her bonds as he carries her into the house, flicking on a lamp and flooding the old room with light. It is threadbare, a moth-eaten couch in the corner and an old rug at his feet, all manner of trash and old papers scattered across the floorboards. He throws the girl onto the couch and raises a dirty finger to his lips. She stares at him, her eyes so blue and full of innocence, as he reaches to her and pulls the tape from her mouth.

She instantly screams, filling the old room with a piercing screech.

"Shh!" he growls, grabbing her and putting a hand over her mouth. "Did I tell you to do that? Shut up! Now!"

The scream dies as she breaths into his palm, her chest

heaving and her eyes wide with terror. Satisfied, the man leans away from her, his eyes moving over her skirt and slender legs to where her ankles are tied together with rope, to her shirt and the blonde curls sitting on her shoulders. She breathes hard, her lips trembling as they press together, residue from the tape still sticking on the skin around her lips. She inhales sharply, whimpering as he reaches to caress her hair.

Enjoying the terror on her face, he gets up from the couch and heads for the kitchen, kicking papers and old food containers out of his way. The countertops are covered in dirty dishes, mold, and buzzing flies on the pots. It stinks of old tobacco and moldy food in here.

As he leaves, the girl works on the rope at her wrists. She got them fairly loose during her hellish journey in the truck over here, listening to the rumble of the engine as this evil man took her farther and farther from her home. Now the rope is almost loose. Gritting her teeth, she wriggles her slim wrists until one of them comes free.

In the kitchen, the kidnapper pulls open a kitchen drawer with a wooden scrape. It may once have been white, but the paint has chipped and dirtied so badly it's almost black. He pulls out a kitchen knife, examining the blade in the meager lamplight.

The girl jumps with fright as a sudden loud bang comes from the kitchen, shattering the silence.

"Ahhh!" the man gives a primal scream, slamming the knife's handle on the ground and shaking the whole house. "I told you to listen! I told you not to scream! Now you'll pay."

He slams his boot on the floor in a fit of rage. "Why must you make me do this? I don't like hurting little girls."

He stomps back to the living room as the girl quickly pulls the rope back around her wrists, sitting still like a statue, breathing hard in horror as the monster rushes for her. He stops in the living room, chest heaving as he glares at her, the lamplight spilling dusty yellow light on his enormous silhouette. For a moment, he stares down at her in silence. The girl looks to the ceiling, her heart pounding with fear as she wills herself not to cry.

Her whole body jolts as he slams his boot on the floorboards again, making a mighty booming sound.

"That's it!" he roars. "I've had it with you!"

She flinches, but he turns from her and heads for the hallway, pulling up an old rug obscuring a trapdoor and throwing it aside. His boots stomp on the basement steps as he descends, pulling on a cord that switches on a dusty old bulb. Cobwebs hang in the corners, and the scent of dirt and body odor clings to everything.

Several old boxes litter the corners, and a dark bloodstain is on the floor, dried and brown. The man's boot hits one of the many chains, and it drags on the floor with a slither of metal.

There's a weak groan as he approaches, the dusty light falling on three teenage girls lying on the ground with their legs chained to the walls. They're skinny and dirty, all weak and malnourished.

One girl is slumped on the floor, her tangled hair over her face. She's wearing a dress, and it's so dirty it's impossible to tell its original color.

The girl in the center scrambles away from the kidnapper, the chains clinking as she shifts away, not looking at him.

The third teenager is glaring at the man with hate. Her face is dirty, her hair a knotted mess. There's silence save for the clinking of chains and their ragged breathing.

"You killed her," whispers the girl, pointing at the lifeless body on the ground.

#

Upstairs, the young girl scrambles to loosen the rope around her wrists, tears of terror burning in her eyes. Her arms free, she attacks the dry rope around her ankles, not caring that it hurts her fingers. This room stinks of old food and blood, and she's never been so terrified in all her life. Throwing the rope to the floor, she runs to the door, praying she isn't making too much noise. She turns the knob.

It doesn't open. It rattles as she pulls it but doesn't budge.

"Oh God!" she sobs. "Please, help me!"

She runs past the hallway and into the kitchen. She stops in horror when she comes to the kitchen door boarded up with planks of wood and rusty nails. A dry sob crawls up her throat.

I need to get out of here!

#

The kidnapper moves to the slumped-over girl on the floor. She's pale and corpse-thin. He moves the hair from her face; her skin is almost blue. She's so skinny her ribs are showing, her hip bones protruding. Her skin is frigid, already in the throes of rigor mortis.

The man chuckles. "You see, this is what happens to little girls who don't listen."

The nearby girl growls. "I hate you!" She collapses against the wall, tears leaving dirty streaks down her face. "I just want my mom."

"You'll get your mommy, alright," says the guy, getting to his feet. The girl screams, cowering away as he approaches…

#

At the same moment, the kidnapped girl snatches up an ax from beside the sofa. Maybe the guy used it to chop wood to board up the doors. She slams it against the nearest window, making a massive crack in the glass, her breaths coming in ragged and fast as fear spills ice-cold through her belly. He could come back at any moment. Muscles burning, groaning with excursion, she hits the glass again, and it explodes in an almost musical crash of shattering glass. Terrified, she throws the ax to the side and scrambles through the window, crying out as glass sticks into her legs and hands. Sharp, burning agony tears across her leg as she scrambles through.

She collapses onto the drying grass, sobbing, stinging pain lacing up her limbs as she gets to her feet, trembling from head to foot. She looks around, then down at her hands, where shards of glass are sticking into her skin, dripping crimson. The pain ebbs through her body, but she can't stop now. That evil man is coming.

She takes off running, heading for the woods, heart screaming as she flees for her young life.

#

"Damn it!" the kidnapper hisses, reappearing on the first floor, his shirt covered in fresh blood. He glances at the discarded ropes on the ground, his eyes traveling to the ax and the broken window. "Where are you?"

The cool air hits his face as he unlocks the front door and marches outside. The wind rustles the trees, his truck sitting close by. He heads to the window with its broken glass stained red. The blonde girl is nowhere to be seen, but a trail of blood shimmers in the moonlight at his feet.

She ran off into the woods. On his powerful legs, he runs across the field and towards the dark trees.

#

The girl can hear him gaining on her, spiking fresh fear through her as she stumbles on her tattered legs, panic stabbing at her heart, hot blood running down her legs. She can barely see anything, the darkness wanting to swallow her whole as she runs over twigs and stones, loose branches hitting her face and arms as she maneuvers through the trees.

With a cry, she suddenly trips over a boulder, twisting her ankle on the way down. Throwing out her bleeding hands, she lets out a terrified scream as she tumbles down the hill, hitting rocks and stones on the way down. A sudden sharp pain explodes in her skull, and the girl lies still with a soft groan.

#

The kidnapper stands above the girl, her shirt in ruins, cuts and blood all over her body from her little scramble through the window. She's landed beside a lake at the bottom of the hill, her motionless hand in the water as she lies there, a deep gash on her temple. He kneels before her, gently turning her head and examining the cut.

"Stupid kid," he says softly. "Why'd you run, huh?"

#

Jasmine groans as the alarm blares on her bedside table. *Such an obnoxious noise, damn!* She'd forgotten to deactivate it last night.

Her arm extends from the blue satin comforter and shuts off the incessant ringing. She rubs her face, grimacing at the morning sunlight. She looks up at the ceiling and lets the stress settle on her shoulders. Barely a moment later, her cell phone rings, making her groan.

"Hello," she sighs into the receiver, not caring how tired her voice sounds.

"Hi, Mom."

Blinking awake, Jasmine sits up. "Hey, my honey bunches of oats," she says, smiling at her daughter's voice. It's an old nickname of theirs.

"Dad and I are gonna have brunch this morning,"

"Brunch, huh?" she asks. *Fancy.*

"Yeah. Would you like to join us? Me, you, and Dad," she sounds so happy. Discomfort squirms in Jasmine's guts. She's still a little bitter that she hasn't seen Mercari since the previous morning, but it's good to hear her voice.

"Honey, don't you think you and your father should spend some quality time together?"

"Nothing's better than spending time with *both* my parents," says Mercari.

Jasmine supposes she can't argue with that. "Okay. Let Mommy get herself together," she says, stretching as she throws off her blanket.

"Great!" she sounds delighted. "You can meet us at my favorite place, okay?"

"Sure, honey. I'll be there soon."

Twenty minutes later, Jasmine's showered and dressed, grabbing her keys and purse before opening her front door. She screams in fright at the man standing on her doorstep.

"Oh gosh, Taylor, you scared me," she cries, clutching her chest.

Taylor's eyes sparkle with amusement as he holds up a coffee in one hand, a bunch of roses in the other. "Sorry, I was going to knock. I thought I'd drop by, maybe try and ease your mind a little bit from last night?"

"Oh, Taylor, that's so sweet of you," Jasmine babbles, edging out of her home and locking the front door. "But I'm on my way out to see my daughter. Sorry."

"No problem," he says. "Take your coffee anyway, I insist. And, uh, these are for you," he holds out the roses.

"Thank you. I appreciate it," she says, hanging her purse on her arm so she can take the flowers. "You're so sweet."

"I'd better get going, anyway," says Taylor, gesturing with his thumb over to his shoulder to where his car is parked. "Why don't you call me later?"

"Will do," she says and waves as Taylor drives off. She smiles at the flowers and the warm coffee in her hand, feeling the sun on her face. As she's making her way to the garage, she spots something on the ground.

It's a bracelet, pink and green. "That's odd," she mutters, tucking the roses under her arm and bending to pick it up. *Mercari's always losing things.* She'll have to remember to give it back to her at brunch.

#

A few minutes later, she's pulling up at a cute little restaurant shaped like a house painted bright yellow, reminding Jasmine of a beachside place. Mercari and Kel are sitting outside at a table, and Mercari leaps to her feet as she spots her mother. "Mom! You're here!"

Jasmine chuckles. For all her pretense that she's all grown up already, Mercari still acts like a little kid at times.

"Hey, baby," she says happily as Mercari's arms wrap around her in a hug.

"Hey," says Kel, waving as he gets to his feet. Grinning, he holds out his arms as well. Despite her lingering annoyance at taking her daughter away the day before, Jasmine giggles. With the surprise gifts from Taylor and the good weather, it's hard to be in a bad mood.

"Hi," she says, briefly hugging her ex.

"You look gorgeous as always," he says warmly as he pulls out a chair for her.

"Thank you," she looks down to hide her burning cheeks as Mercari watches with wide eyes.

"It's good to see you," he presses. "I'm glad you could make it."

"Mom, be nice," says Mercari, who's grinning as she takes a seat beside her dad.

She doesn't answer, busying herself with folding a napkin in her lap. *Why's he so nice to me all of a sudden?*

"I mean it," he says, resting his warm hand on top of hers.

Jasmine regards him with a slight smile, wondering about this switch in behavior.

"I have to go to the restroom, you guys," says Mercari, getting to her feet.

"Alright, baby."

#

None of them notice the old black truck with chipped paint pulling up in the near distance. A man looks in Kel's direction, watching the family with interest. His dark brown eyes follow Mercari, who makes her way to the other side of the building. He steps out of his vehicle, taking a deep puff of his cigarette before crushing the tip under his cowboy boot.

He adjusts his hat and the belt buckle on his blue jeans, glancing over to see the little girl open the side door to the restaurant.

#

"Baby, what happened?" asks Kel, his dark eyes glancing at Jasmine's arm. She looks down as he touches the soft flesh of her forearm, where there's a dark blue bruise.

"Ouch, Kel," she winces, drawing her arm back. "That's funny. I don't know what happened. I'm fine," she insists, growing impatient at Kel's worried look. "And enough of the sweet talk. I'm not your 'baby.'"

Kel sighs, leaning back in his chair. There's a light breeze today, blowing several fall leaves beneath the bench at their feet. "I can't apologize enough for the damage I caused," he says quietly. "I just… I truly hope you can find it in your heart to forgive me."

Neither of them takes any notice of the heavy footsteps passing their table.

"Hey, you alright?" asks Kel as Jasmine looks into the distance, fidgeting with her hair.

"Jasmine?"

"I've just been exhausted lately," she confesses, feeling the weight of work and responsibilities heavy on her shoulders. "It's like… I'm so drained. All I want to do is sleep. I don't know, Kel… with all these kidnappings of young girls going on, I think I'm tired and scared. I've got all these emotions running through me all the time, and I don't know what to do…" her voice cracks as she puts her hand on her forehead, feeling dizzy and miserable all at once. The stress never ends. It just piles up more and more on her until she feels on the verge of splintering.

"Jas, Jas. Hey, it's okay. Listen, you have to take it easy," says Kel gently, "and tend to yourself. You're always so wrapped up in your work. Don't forget. We have a child that needs her parents."

That annoys her. "Kel, I'm not about to hear another lecture from you."

"You don't like to hear the truth," he grumbles, leaning away from her. "That's the reason why we separated."

"That's not the reason, Kel, and you know it."

Exhaustion clashes with anger. She isn't in the mood for yet another fight.

#

Mercari, back from her trip to the bathroom, is looking at the display of cupcakes. They're all so cute.

Maybe she can convince her mom or dad to get her a chocolate chip one before they leave.

A light touch on her shoulder startles her, and she turns and looks up at a large man wearing a cowboy hat. He raises a bushy eyebrow at her.

"Would you like a cupcake? They sure look tasty."

Mercari looks at him in silence.

#

"Listen, Kel, I really can't do this right now," Jasmine pleads. "We need to focus on keeping our daughter safe."

"I think it's time to get her a cellphone," he says, looking at her. "She's been asking for one for a while now."

Jasmine lets out a frustrated sigh. "I know, I know." She doesn't want to think of Mercari with a cellphone. All those apps and websites can be so dangerous.

"Why do you say it like that?"

"Well, you know how I feel about cellphones," Jasmine folds her arms.

"I agree," he says, "But I also understand the importance of having one."

#

"Oh God," blurts Jasmine, her eyes widening. "Where's Mercari?"

They both leap to their feet, staring dumbly at the chair she vacated. How long has she been gone? Ten minutes? Longer?

"Mercari!" Jasmine screams as they dart through the glass double doors of the restaurant, ignoring the startled looks of customers and staff. Jasmine rushes straight for the restroom; there are only two stalls, and they're both empty. Her stomach plummets. She's not here.

"Oh my God, where's my baby?" Jasmine cries.

Kel's outside, speaking to others in the diner in a rapid voice, met with shaking heads and shrugs.

The room spins around Jasmine as her chest tightens, flashes of the *Missing* posters bursting in her mind. "Where is my child?" she whispers, clutching her head. Kel glances up at her, fear like nothing she's seen in his face before sending fresh panic washing over her in crashing waves. Something catches her eye in the parking lot, and they both glance outside.

There's a truck, a large man closing the door on a dark-haired girl bundled inside.

#

"Mercari!" Kel bellows, nearly knocking over a waitress and her tray as he bursts out of the restaurant, Jasmine at his heels. The truck's engine rumbles to life as they run towards it, their breaths fast and hard, panic igniting their footsteps.

"Hey! HEY!" Kel bellows, running into the side of the truck and pummeling it with his fists. The truck rocks as the man stares from inside in astonishment.

"Let my daughter go, you miserable creep!" Ken yells. Jasmine reaches the vehicle, pounding on it too.

"That's my daughter in there! Let her out now! I'll kill you!" shouts Kel, yanking on the handle of the truck door. The girl in the back seat looks out at them. Calm and curious.

"Mom, Dad? What are you doing?"

They spin around and see Mercari, perfectly safe, staring at them both.

"Oh my God. My baby," Jasmine gasps, running over to pull Mercari into her arms. The girl inside the truck, dark-haired but looking nothing like Mercari really, sips on her drink as she stares at Kel in silence.

The man climbs out of his truck as Kel backs away, his hands on his head. "I'm so, so sorry," he mumbles. "I don't know what happened…." He can't think of the right words to say. Embarrassment flushes hot through him. He's never felt so foolish. His heart is still hammering at a million miles an hour.

"That's quite alright," said the man. He's an older guy with graying stubble and a baseball cap. "I just don't understand what happened."

"It's just… well, with all the abductions lately," says Kel weakly, knowing no number of excuses can pardon what he just did. "Our daughter didn't come back from the bathroom, and we thought…" his voice trails off. "I apologize. We panicked."

The man squints at Kel, reaching in his shirt pocket to pull out a pair of glasses. His eyes widen in recognition once the spectacles are on his nose. "Kel? Is that you?"

"Excuse me?"

"It's me, Mason," says the man, stepping forward with a smile and extending his hand. "From Plant Co. We used to work together a while back before the place was shut down. Do you remember?"

As the adrenaline fades and Kel starts to see clearly again, familiarity washes over him at the man's weathered, friendly face. "Mason. Right, of course," says Kel, shaking the man's hand. "I'm so embarrassed." He gives a shy grin, lowering his head. "I'm sorry if I startled you."

"No need for that," Mason waves a hand. "I understand. So much has been going on in Grandville recently. It's why I keep my granddaughter close." He gestures to the little girl in his truck, who's leaning back in her seat, headphones in her ears.

"Yeah. Well, I better let you two get going," says Kel. "Maybe we'll see each other again on a better note." Shame still prickles through him.

"You can most definitely count on it," smiles Mason.
Kel takes a deep breath, glancing back to see Jasmine
hugging a confused Mercari close.

None of them feel like eating anymore after that
display. Everyone in the restaurant must think they're crazy.
Instead, Kel lets Mercari into his car and watches as she
clambers in. The window is slightly open, allowing in fresh
air.

"Wait, Kel! I forgot something," says Jasmine,
catching up to them out of breath. Her cheeks are flushed as
she holds up a bracelet in her fingers. "Here, Mercari, you
must have dropped this earlier."

"Uh, that's not mine," says her daughter, making a
face.

"Oh," says Jasmine. "I found it in our yard. I figured
you dropped it."

"Sorry, Mom. I've never owned a bracelet like that."

"Well, okay," Jasmine deposits the bracelet into her

purse. "I'll see you guys later."

#

Nighttime falls as a truck parks across the street from Jasmine and Mercari's home, the lights flickering off as the engine rumbles into silence. Oblivious, Jasmine finishes tying up her tangle of dark curls into an elegant bun on top of her head. She's wearing a pink robe and matching slippers, and when her cell phone rings, she snatches it up.

"Mercari's sleeping, Kel."

"There's no need to be so upset when you hear my voice," says her ex, sounding torn between amusement and exasperation.

#

The truck driver pulls out a pair of binoculars and focuses on Jasmine's house, spotting the flicker of a pink robe as she paces, saying something he can't hear on her phone. His sights move to the bedroom on the second floor; all the lights are out.

#

"Listen, Jasmine. I bought Mercari a cell phone today."

Jasmine stops pacing, sucking in breath through her teeth.

"And you just thought to mention it now, at this time of night?" she demands.

She hears Kel sigh on the line. "I'm sorry. I hung out with Mason tonight and just got back. I learned a lot from that guy when we worked together."

There's silence as Jasmine remembers with a flutter of shame in her stomach the embarrassing display at the restaurant today.

"I can bring it by tonight if you like."

"I don't think that's a good idea. We can just pick it up tomorrow. Just be thankful I'm not upset. You still went behind my back to get her a cellphone even though I repeatedly said I wasn't comfortable with it."

"You're right," Kel chuckles. There's a pause. "You know I won't give up on my family, Jasmine."

She sighs, rubbing the bridge of her nose. "Please, Kel. Not now."

"If not now, then when?"

#

The man clambers out of the truck, wearing all black. Looking around and noting that the street, alight with streetlamps, is empty, he crosses towards the house, pulling a hood over his head.

#

"You want to talk about it? Fine," says Jasmine, and despite herself, her voice cracks. "You really hurt me, you know."

"I do know. I can't apologize enough."

#

The man stands in the yard in the shadow of a tree, watching Jasmine through the window on the kitchen door, eyes sliding to her waist where the soft material of the dressing gown hugs her curvy frame.

#

A loud knock on the door startles Jasmine, and she lets out a sharp gasp.

"You okay?"

"Yeah, someone's at my door."

"At this time of night?" Kel echoes her thoughts.

"Listen, I've got to go. I'll see you tomorrow," says Jasmine and hangs up, frowning. She places the cell phone on the marble countertop and approaches the door. She hesitates. There's no one there, and it's too dark to see.

"Hello?" she calls into the darkness as she unlocks the door. "Is someone there?"

She steps out onto the cement of the outside, the cold breeze like ice on her legs, making her shiver. She steps out, curiosity filling her as she folds her arms against the cold of the night. Someone *definitely* knocked on her door just now. She scans the yard, and there's a sudden slam behind her as her door closes.

"Oh, God!" Jasmine darts back to her door and tries to yank it open, but it's locked. Not just closed like last time, but *locked*!

Her heart seizes in terror as she spots a man on the other side, wearing all black, still and silent, inside her home.

She bangs her fist on the door as he watches in silence. "Let me in!" she cries in a panic. "Please don't hurt my baby. I'll give you anything you want!"

The man slowly turns and disappears from her sight.

"No! NO!" she screams. She runs to the other side of the house, grabbing the window to the living room and trying to pull it open, but it won't budge. She locked them all.

"God, please help me!" she cries out. Her cell phone is in the kitchen. Why was she stupid enough to leave it there?

"Mercari!" Jasmine yells. She darts back to the kitchen door with its glass window, snatching up a nearby rock as her chest heaves with fright. She's never been so scared in all her life.

#

Mercari slowly wakes up as she hears a strange sound coming from outside. Maybe it's the wind. Rubbing her eyes, the little girl sits up in bed when she hears her mother shout her name.

"Mercari! MERCARI!"

"Mom?"

Mercari throws off the blanket and slips her feet into the slippers by her bed, oblivious to the man standing quietly in the corner, watching. She checks out of the window but sees nothing except her yard, the howling wind blowing at the skeletal trees.

Shivering, Mercari closes the curtains.

The man slips around the corner a millisecond before Mercari turns.

The little girl ventures to the hallway, flicking on the light. She goes to her mother's room to tell her about the strange shouting, but her mother's not in her bed. There's a sudden banging noise downstairs, making Mercari jump. She feels like a toddler again, suddenly frightened and alone.

"Mom?" she asks, tears slipping down her cheeks. "Are you okay?"

Bravely, she tiptoes down the stairs, slippers slapping on the carpet, and finds her mother on the other side of the kitchen door outside, panic written all over her face. The window's been shattered, and her mother has stuck her arm through, trying to reach the handle.

"Mercari, baby!" Jasmine cries as soon as Mercari opens the door, wrapping her up in a tight hug.

#

The flashing blue and red lights of the police car

make Jasmine feel a lot safer. She hasn't let Mercari out of her sight, and even now, they're standing shivering in the yard, a policewoman with a pen and pad giving them a sympathetic look.

"Well, ma'am, we've checked your house from top to bottom," she says. She's a middle-aged lady with blonde hair in a tight bun, her blue eyes tired looking, almost jaded. "We checked every room and every closet, and there's no one there. Your house is empty."

"But there was someone there," says Jasmine, her iron grip on Mercari not yielding. "He locked me out! How do you explain that?"

"I believe you," says the cop. "He might have gotten away. Look, if you see anything else strange, feel free to give us a call. God knows we have to be more careful these days." Her blue eyes slide to Mercari. Jasmine sniffles, nodding as the policewoman writes her number and her name, Kathleen Rivers.

There's the sound of an approaching car engine, and a vehicle pulls up. "Daddy!" Mercari cries, wriggling out of her mother's arms.

"Mercari!"

She's already hugging Kel, who holds her close.

"That's her father," says Jasmine, clearing her throat as Kel comes over, hand in hand with Mercari.

"Are you okay?" he asks, rubbing her back.

"Well, we've searched the whole house, and it's all clear of intruders," says Officer Rivers. She glances back at the house. "As I told your wife, please give us a call if you notice anything else strange. We'll be patrolling the area."

Part of Jasmine feels foolish. She's overreacted so much lately. But she'd bet her life there was someone here tonight, and even if she somehow hallucinated, how could she explain being locked out of her house?

Something was wrong. She could feel it.

#

"Honey, come eat your breakfast. We'll be late!" Jasmine calls on Monday morning, trying to pour cereal and pull on her white heels simultaneously. She buttons up her green dress as toast pops out of the toaster, sliding her feet properly into her shoes.

"Coming, Mom."

Doing up the last button, Jasmine hurries to the fridge and pours juice into the glasses on the table. Mercari appears in the doorway, hands behind her back and a smile on her face.

"You look cheery," says Jasmine.

"I have a surprise for you," says Mercari, swaying like she's got a secret.

"Hmm, well, let me think," says Jasmine. "Is it Christmas already? Did I forget?"

"No," Mercari giggles, brown eyes sparkling.

"Well, it's not my birthday," Jasmine taps her chin. She darts to her daughter and tickles her tummy, making her shriek with laughter and wriggle away.

"No tickling, Mom! I'm in the seventh grade!"

"You're never too old for a tickle," says Jasmine, looking down at her daughter. She's so beautiful and sweet.

"Here," says Mercari, handing an envelope to her mother.

"Well, what have we here?"

"Go ahead, read it aloud!" says Mercari, sliding onto a chair at the dining table and pulling her cereal to her.

Jasmine opens and reads the letter.

"*Mom, there is no one in this entire world like you. You're a superhero without a cape. You rescue me when I'm in trouble and sometimes when I'm not. You're so brave, and I can't imagine life without you. You're my world, my mommy, who takes care of me. I appreciate you. Words can't express how I feel. I love you so much, Mom.* Aww, baby," Jasmine's eyes have filled with tears, and one rolls down her cheek as she wraps her arms around her daughter, holding her close and inhaling her soft, sweet child's smell. "I love you to the moon and back. I'm so blessed to be your mommy."

#

The school morning rush commences, teachers hurrying down corridors with folders clutched to chests, students hanging outside doing last-minute homework or sharing earphones, glancing up now and then at the overcast sky-threatening rain. Jasmine's car pulls up near the school's front

of chattering and laughing teenagers and smiles at her daughter.

"Well, kiddo, you have a wonderful day today, okay? You

think we might hit the mall after school?"

"Yeah, shopping. I love it," Mercari grins.

A crackle of thunder suddenly sounds above them. A couple

of girls outside gave playful screams as kids on benches jump up to

hurry inside, shoving textbooks and stationery into their bags.

"You better hurry inside. It might rain soon."

"Later, Mom."

Jasmine blows her a kiss.

#

Among the family cars and vehicles, a truck pulls up outside

the school. The driver smokes a cigarette, the end flaring amber, as

they watch the thirteen-year-old girl with a tangle of black curls

wave goodbye to her mother. She catches up with her friends, and

they exchange delighted giggles and high-fives.

#

"We were wondering when you'd get here," says Carmen, a

pale girl with long, blonde hair, adjusting the strap on her backpack.

Kathy, a curly-haired girl, links her arm through Mercari's, her other arm leaden with books. "Come on, we've got so much to catch you up on."

They all gasp when cold, thick raindrops fall from the sky, instantly drenching them.

"Inside, please, everyone!" shouts a teacher from the doorway. "Hurry!"

Pulling up hoodies or covering their heads with their bags, the students run giggling into the school.

#

The person pulls on their hoodie as the rain falls harder. All the students go inside knowing that the doors will automatically lock once they're closed. The spy takes off at a sprint, boots pounding heavily on the concrete as the rain falls in a thunderous downpour. The last student slides through the doors, and they slowly close. The following person grasps the door handle at the last moment and slips inside. Nobody looks back to notice them. People are lost in chatting with their friends or finding their classrooms. The person shakes off some of the water from their hoodie, leaning against the wall. Along the corridor, two teachers are lost in their conversation, laughing.

#

"Okay, okay. What's this 'catching up' I've got to do?" Mercari asks.

Kathy pulls something out of her backpack, excitement all over her face. Mercari's jaw drops open as she looks at the phone in her friend's hand.

"Oh my God, your parents got you a phone?" Mercari asks, unable to hide the envy from her voice.

"Yes, finally! It only took them a million years!" says Kathy. "My dad kept whining about how a girl my age doesn't need one. He's totally living in the ice age."

The girls giggle. Carmen pulls out her phone, and they put them side by side, comparing.

#

A teacher turns to join her class and notices a person in black watching a small group of seventh-grade girls. Frowning and wondering if they're one of the parents who've gotten lost, she approaches, her heels clacking on the floor.

"Mrs. Turner?" she feels a tap on her shoulder. "Could you please check my paper before I hand it in? I'm so bad with spelling."

"Yes, of course," says the teacher, turning to smile at the timid mousy-haired girl clutching her homework to her chest. "Run along into class, and I'll meet you there in a moment."

When Mrs. Turner turns back to the corridor, the person in black is gone.

#

"It's *your* turn to get a phone, friend," says Carmen, waving her cell in Mercari's face.

"Girls," says a stern voice. Carmen gives a startled squeak as she and Kathy hide their phones behind their backs.

Mrs. Turner raises an eyebrow, which is white like

her hair. "I saw those phones, girls. Make sure they're away in your bags before class."

"Please, Mrs. Turner, it's too early for a lecture," moans Kathy.

"I'm not worried about the phones, really," says the teacher. "I'd like to know who that person was behind you a moment ago. One of your parents?"

The girls all shake their heads. They were so engrossed in their conversation they didn't notice anyone. "Sorry, Mrs. Turner, but we didn't see anybody."

"Okay, girls," Mrs. Turner sighs, her hands planting on her hips as the students around them hurry to class, still chattering and giggling. "Get to class, then. And no cell phone usage in class, or they'll be confiscated!" she calls after them.

"Yes, ma'am," calls Kathy, and they all snicker. Mrs. Turner marches off with a clack of her heels.

#

Dripping water onto the floor, the person in the black hoodie enters through the back door, watching Mrs. Turner disappear into her class.

"Hello, there," says a bright voice. "Can I help you?"

They take a deep breath and turn to see a friendly-looking older Caucasian lady with a green shirt and eyeglasses hanging on her neck. She's extended her hand for a handshake, but they don't extend their hand back.

"Uh, yeah."

"What is it I can help you with?" she asks. "I'm Jane Trahan, the librarian."

The spy takes out a soggy brown paper bag and hands it to her. "This is Mercari's lunch. She forgot it this morning."

Mrs. Trahan's smile becomes fixed as she holds the wet bag at arm's length. "Mercari who, honey?"

"Mercari Johnson. She's in the seventh grade."

"Well, it might be a wet lunch," says the librarian, giving a nervous laugh. The person starts to walk away, and she calls after them, "Wait! I'm sorry. You never told me your name?"

They swallow a sigh and turn back to the nosey Mrs. Jane, plastering a smile on their face. "A friend of the family."

#

The reporting office is bedlam. Phones ring, a teleprompter is running, and the rustle of papers and hiss of the coffee machine is a cacophony of noise. Jasmine grimaces, pouring herself a cup of coffee.

Warm hands slide onto her shoulders, massaging away the ache kindling at the top of her back. "Oh, Taylor, if you start, I won't let you stop," she groans in pleasure at his thumbs, kneading the sore muscles near her neck.

"It doesn't have to," Taylor murmurs in her ear, planting a playful kiss on her ear that makes her giggle, goosebumps springing up on her neck. "How about we have dinner tonight?"

"That'd be nice," she says slowly. "But..."

"But what?"

Jasmine turns to face him. "Shelby's coming over to work on some reports later."

"Well, I'm up for a late evening if you are," his hands slid down her arms until their fingers were entwined. "Maybe a glass of champagne?" he adds, his dark eyebrows rising, making her smile.

"Sounds good to me," she brightens up. *Champagne sounds nice.*

Someone clears their throat nearby. Shelby is standing a few feet away.

"You look gorgeous today, Shelby," says Jasmine, greeting her coworker with a bright smile.

Shelby smiles and does a spin. She's wearing a white business suit with a dark blue shirt and a gold necklace, her dark hair curled and resting on her shoulders. "Well, thank you, honey."

"She's right. You're looking sharp," says Taylor and takes a sip from his mug.

"Thank you, Taylor. So, are we still on for this evening, Jasmine?" she helps herself to some coffee.

"Of course."

"Excuse me, guys," says a man holding a manila

folder in his large hand. Rick has short dark hair and is wearing a striped suit. "Jasmine, there's a phone call for you."

"Can you take a message?" Jasmine asks anxiously. She doesn't feel like talking to anyone on the phone right now. With things happening at home and the scare from the other night, her stress levels are high.

"It's Mercari's school."

"Oh," Jasmine sets down her coffee on the nearest desk. "Oh gosh."

#

Light rain is still falling when Jasmine is buzzed into the school. The floor is damp, a yellow *CAUTION. WET FLOOR* sign perched near the wall. Jasmine didn't bring an umbrella, and damp clings to her hair.

"Mercari?" Jasmine says, entering the office. Her daughter is there, talking to the receptionist.

"Mom," says Mercari, clutching a damp paper bag. She holds it up. "You really brought me a wet sandwich for lunch?"

"I thought you grabbed your lunch from the counter this

morning, sweetie," says Jasmine, confused. She steps closer to Mercari. She doesn't recognize the bag. "Give me that."

She takes the bag and looks at the receptionist. "Maybe someone gave this to my child by accident?"

"They specifically said it was for your daughter," says the receptionist. "They gave it to the librarian this morning."

"They? Who's they?" Jasmine demands. "Does anyone know who brought this? Was it her father?"

"Dad wouldn't give me a wet bag," Mercari mumbles.

The lady behind the desk takes off her glasses. "Now, let's all calm down. I'm sure there's a reasonable explanation for all this."

Another woman appears, an older lady wearing a green shirt, a pair of glasses hanging on a chain around her neck.

"This is Mrs. Trahan, the librarian. She brought in the lunch, so I'm sure she can solve this."

"Is everything okay?" asks Mrs. Trahan, blinking.

"Can you help us? Nothing is getting solved with these two," snaps Jasmine, gesturing to Mercari and the receptionist. She bristles, but at that moment, Jasmine doesn't much care.

"How may I help?" asks the librarian politely, perching the glasses on her nose and giving Mercari a warm smile.

They quickly explain, and the librarian frowns for a moment. "Well, yes. She said she was a family friend and she was here to drop off Mercari's lunch. Mercari Johnson in the seventh grade. That's you, isn't it, dear?" she gives the little girl another friendly smile.

Silence falls across the room as Jasmine and Mercari stare at each other. A familiar flicker of fear beats in Jasmine's heart.

#

Jasmine pulls on her heel and reaches for the earrings on her dresser when the doorbell rings downstairs.

"Mercari! Could you get the door, honey?" she calls as she puts the earring in, looking into the dresser.

"Okay, Mom."

When Jasmine's done brushing her hair, she shouts, "Who was it?"

Silence greets her.

"Mercari?"

Jasmine lays down her brush, a prickle of fear running down her spine. She descends the stairs. "Cari?"

No one's in the living room, and the front door is wide open. *Oh, God.* She runs towards the door, and someone suddenly jumps into the doorway, making her scream.

"Oh, Lord!" Jasmine breathes, clutching her chest. "For God's sake, Shelby!"

Shelby giggles. "I'm sorry, girl," she says, though she doesn't look sorry at all.

"Where's Mercari?"

Her daughter is outside, Kel smiling behind her. She's jumping for joy.

"Mom, check it out! Dad got me a cell phone!"

Jasmine's heart rate slows, and she lets out a burst of

breath. She's starting to get paranoid.

She stands frozen in place as Mercari bounces over, happiness shining on her young face. She waves the phone box at her. It's not the latest phone, but it's a decent model. Jasmine's insides squirm uncomfortably. "Isn't it awesome, Mom?"

"Yes, honey, it is," Jasmine forces a smile, recovering.

"Uh, actually, it's from both of us," says Kel, winking at Jasmine.

"Thank you, guys! Oh, I can't wait to open it," Mercari chatters happily.

Shelby watches with a smile, and Jasmine invites them in. "It's good to see you again, Kel," says Shelby, shaking his hand.

"Can I open it? I'll die if I don't get to open it," Mercari wails, making them all laugh.

"Come on, I'll help you," says Shelby, guiding the little girl into the house. Kel and Jasmine look at each other. Jasmine still isn't comfortable with Mercari having a phone, but she supposes it can't be helped. She smiles at Kel as his eyes flicker from her new heels to her sparkling earrings.

"Wow, you look beautiful."

"Thank you," she looks at the ground. The grass is still damp from the day's rain, and the last of the fall leaves have been dampened to mush.

Kel chuckles. "You know, after all these years, you're still shy."

"I'm not," she lifts her chin, her cheeks burning. "I'm a reporter!" she giggles.

"You know what I mean," Kel says, taking a step closer to her. He has this funny smile on his face that, for some reason, really *does* make her feel suddenly bashful. "Shy around me."

It gets quiet, a gentle breeze blowing Kel's sweater, his warm brown eyes gazing at her. Then he sighs and looks away, and the spell is broken. "You're dressed up, so I guess you have a date?"

"Yes, I do," she blinks. "I better get ready —"

Kel takes her hand as she turns, gently pulling her so she's facing him. Neither of them notices Shelby watching from the living room window. "Listen, Jas. I love you, and Mercari too. I know what I did was wrong, and I can't apologize enough."

The discomfort returns, the tightening in her chest. Jasmine feels a sudden urge to shove him away.

"Please think about our family. For the sake of our daughter."

"Just like you thought about us when you were messing up, right?" she says sharply. His betrayal still hurts, like a knife twisting in her guts. There's no room left for affection. That's what she tells herself. "You should've thought about that at the time, Kel. Don't put this on me." She tugs her arm from his grip. "I have to go."

Jasmine feels Kel's eyes on her back as she goes inside.

#

Kel sighs through his nose, frustration rippling through him. He hears a car engine and the crunch of tires on the gravel and turns to see a dark-haired man stepping out of a car before Jasmine's home. He looks like a model; tall, olive-skinned, and handsome, wearing a casual button-down shirt and a gray suit jacket. He's holding a bunch of roses, and he frowns slightly as his eyes meet Kel's.

"Hi there," he says as he approaches, locking his car door with his remote-control key.

"You must be the temp," says Kel coldly.

"Uh, come again?"

"I believe you heard me the first time."

"Yeah. Sure," Taylor smirks a little, brushing past Kel. Bristling, Kel grabs Taylor by the wrist. The man glances at him with a calm expression.

"Don't get it twisted," Kel demands as Taylor yanks his arm from his grip, walking off.

There's a shadow at the window upstairs, and Kel glances up to see Shelby watching from the upper floor window. He sighs hard and turns away, anger and shame mingling in him.

#

"Thanks again for everything, Shelby. I promise I'll work overtime to get this message across," says Jasmine, taking hold of her friend's hand. "You've truly been a blessing. I appreciate everything you've done for Mercari and me."

She feels her eyes burning and blinks, giving a shy smile.

"No worries, girl. That's what I'm here for," Shelby smiles. Her eyes are glassy, too, and she fans her face with her free hand. "Now go, before my makeup gets ruined. Have fun for me, will ya?"

They hug tightly as Taylor watches from the doorway. Over Jasmine's shoulder, Shelby and Taylor's eyes meet.

"Well," Shelby gives Jasmine a sisterly pat and draws away. "You better get going."

She watches from the front door as Jasmine climbs into the passenger seat of Taylor's car and winks at him. His eyes locked on Shelby. He gets into the car beside Jasmine, and the engine revs.

Mercari, meanwhile, is in bed, playing on her new phone. Shelby slowly twists the knob to the girl's bedroom, not making a sound. She watches her through the tiny crack in the door, then taps softly on the wood.

"Hi! Can I come in?"

"Sure," Mercari sits up in bed on her black and pink

comforter set.

"What are you up to?"

"Just downloading some apps on my new phone," Mercari waves it at her, as though Shelby doesn't already know about it. "I want to call my friends and tell them about it, but I'd rather show it off to them in person."

Shelby holds out her hand, and Mercari hands it over. "What kind of apps?" she asks, scrolling through as she sits beside her.

"Nothing really good yet," says Mercari. "I have to wait and see what Kathy and the others have. I guess I'm a little slow," she laughs. "It feels like I'm the last person on Earth to get a cell phone."

"Well, be sure the apps you download are safe," Shelby reminds her. "You don't want to be the next victim."

Mercari blinks at the tone in Shelby's voice. It's not the gentle caress of a concerned parent figure but dark and menacing. Evil, almost. She says nothing.

Shelby bursts out laughing. "I'm just kidding! Come

on, where's your sense of humor?" she hands back the phone while Mercari gives an awkward giggle.

"I mean, girls *are* vanishing," says Shelby, getting to her feet. "But you've nothing to worry about. You're a good kid who listens to her mother," she smiles down at Mercari, who doesn't answer.

"Well, goodnight," she tucks Mercari in. "Don't let the bed bugs bite."

The little girl is silent as Shelby leaves the room, switching off the light and leaving the door cracked, letting in light from the hallway.

#

Darkness fills the night as a fierce wind blows dust in the yard. Creatures from outside, the buzzing of insects, and the shriek of a coyote a few miles away pierce the darkness. In the old two-story house, a teen girl in a spaghetti strap shirt and blue pajama pants sits on a twin bed, her wrists tied to each pole with thick rope. Her golden blonde hair is wrapped in a bun. Several strands escaped sticking to her sweat-soaked skin.

She doesn't know how long she's been crying. She thumps her head against the wooden headboard, tears dribbling down her cheeks as she moans in the gloomy darkness. "Somebody, help me! Please…"

The old floorboards creak. A second girl tiptoes down the corridor, whispering, "Kelly. Kelly!"

She hears the pained moans and cries coming from a nearby doorway and leans in to listen.

"Kelly, is that you?" she gently knocks on the door.

"Who's there?" the voice sounds so sad; it breaks her heart.

"It's me. Victoria."

"Help me, please!" Kelly screams.

Victoria turns the knob and pushes, but it's locked. "I will, I promise," she calls through the wood. "But I can't open the door."

#

A truck, stained gray with smoke and dust, rumbles down the narrow road. The driver pulls a lighter from his black leather jacket and lights the cigarette at his lips.

#

"Victoria!" Kelly whispers into the dark. "There's a rug in front of the door, can you see it? There's a key under there. I saw the lady put it there. Use it and get me out of here. My arms hurt!"

Victoria pulls aside the old rug before the door. Sure enough, shining in the pale moonlight coming through the window is an old key. She picks it up with trembling fingers, not noticing the truck's headlights outside.

"Victoria? Are you there?"

Victoria picks up the key and straightens, staring at it in her hand as her heart thumps. She glances up and down the dark hallway.

The truck, meanwhile, parks outside the house with a crunch of gravel.

"Yes, I'm here."

"Get me out of here!" Kelly screams.

"Kelly," she presses her ear against the locked door.

"What?"

"I think he's back."

"Hurry up! He'll kill us!"

Victoria's fingers fumble as she shoves the key into the lock.

#

Outside, the man steps out of the truck, whistling. He collects some tools from the trunk and a large canister of gasoline. He glances up at the house; a single lamp burns in the first-floor window, though it doesn't do much to brighten the dingy building.

#

Inside, Victoria has Kelly's arm around her shoulders. The blonde girl is limping, wincing on her injured foot.

"My leg hurts so bad," she groans, tears running down her pale cheeks. "I don't think I can make it."

"Sure, you can," whispers Victoria. The girl is using all her strength to help her friend walk. She's heavy, and she can barely hop along on her good leg. "Here, you stand against the wall and rest while I see which doors I can open."

Kelly slouches against the hallway wall, gasping at the throbbing agony in her ankle as Victoria runs from her, the key clutched tight in her trembling hand. She thrusts the key into the holes of several doors, groaning in frustration when none of them open. Each one has a different lock, is boarded up, or the wood is so rotten that the keys simply won't open anymore. Everywhere she goes, windows have heavy wooden planks nailed across them. She doesn't know which way is out.

A key turns in the lock downstairs, and the girls stare at each other in terror. The door downstairs opens with a familiar creak.

#

The man lays everything across an old wooden table that is barely standing. Flies buzz around his head, and he impatiently swats them away. As he glances up, he sees that a nearby hallway door is ajar.

"Now, what are you girls up to?" he says softly into the darkness, his boots thumping on the floorboards. He softly pushes open the door. The moonlight from outside shows an empty bed, the ropes cut.

#

"Kelly," Victoria whispers. "You sit here in the middle of the floor and hold this."

"What do you mean, sit right here?" Kelly whispers back.

"Here, let me help you." Victoria guides the injured girl to the floor. "I need you to be the distraction."

They can hear him coming. Both girls are terrified, their hearts screaming in their chests. If they're discovered, they're done for.

Victoria presses a spray can into her hands.

"What's this?"

"It's bug spray. I found it. Keep it behind your back. When he comes close to you, spray him in the face with it. You see that lamp?" she points to one of the few light sources in the building. It's switched off now, though the shade is so old and dirty that light would struggle through the thick layer of dust and grime.

Kelly nods, her eyes huge with fright.

"Once you blind him with the spray, I'll hit him over the head with that."

They both start as they hear an angry scream from a few rooms down and something clatter against the wall. "He knows you're not there anymore!" Victoria whispers, frightened tears sliding down her cheeks.

"I'm scared! What if I can't do this?" hisses Kelly. "I can't!"

"You have to have faith," Victoria hugs her friend tightly. They both stink from their captivity, but she doesn't care. Kelly's body trembles in her arms.

Doors bang and heavy footsteps pound the floorboards.

#

"When I catch you girls, I'll kill you!" the man roars.

"Help me!" a girl cries from a nearby room. "Please, someone!"

He follows the voice to another closed door. Inside, Victoria and Kelly give each other fearful glances.

The door opens. Kelly looks up at the man, staring at him

right in the face. Silence descends on them as their eyes meet in the dark.

A grin spreads across the man's face. "There you are."

Kelly sits on her knees, frozen. A tear falls from her eye as her breathing quickens, ragged and scared.

"Looks like you didn't get far after all," says her captor with a chuckle. "What is it, huh? Cat got your tongue?"

He steps into the room, and Kelly finds her voice. "Leave me alone, you creep!"

His face twists in anger. "I'll show you what a creep is."

He closes the space between them in two long strides and reaches for her with dirty hands. Kelly pulls up the spray from behind her; the spray goes right into his eyes.

The man howls in agony as his eyes burn. He covers his face, dropping to his knees. Victoria appears from behind the door and smashes him over the head with the lamp. Kelly screams, backing away as the man crumples in a shower of shattered lamp glass, collapsing to the floor with a groan.

"I'll help you. We have to move fast," says Victoria, dragging the sobbing girl off the floor.

#

The man's still howling, covering his streaming eyes as he rolls on the filthy floor. Victoria's heart thunders in her chest. How long will the spray last? Did she do any damage to that creep at all?

Breathing hard, agony pulsing in Kelly's leg, the pair stagger along the hallway in search of an exit. Through the gaps in the boards nailed to windows, silvery moonlight escapes through the slits, illuminating the dusty air. Too long have they been in this misery. They're escaping tonight. Victoria clings to that hope. If they don't get out of here right now, they're both dead.

"Oh, God!" Kelly cries, glancing behind them. The man is at the doorway, his face like thunder, swaying on his feet as blood runs down from his ear.

"Come on!" Victoria urges, and they find themselves in the kitchen. The tools are strewn across the old table, cabinets filthy and covered in grime.

"Rest here. I'll find a door that'll open," Victoria pushes Kelly onto a nearby chair and pulls her arm from her neck. She can move faster on her own.

"Hurry!" Kelly cries.

Victoria runs to the front door, expecting it to be locked, but it opens when she yanks it. For a moment, she blinks in surprise.

"Victoria, what are you doing in there?" Kelly's voice whispers through the darkness. "He's coming!"

Victoria blinks, snapping back to reality. She runs to help her up, and they head for the exit. A cold wind blows in, smelling of freedom. They stagger to the door, hope in their hearts, and see…

Three vans, bright headlights almost blinding them, drive towards the house, tires crunching on the gravel, engines roaring as they get closer. The girls glance at each other.

"Who's that?" Kelly whispers.

"Help!" Victoria screams, waving with her free arm. Surely, it's the cops or someone who's finally discovered this hellish place. "Please, help us!"

"Victoria," Kelly pants beside her, wincing at the pain in her leg. "I don't think this is help."

Victoria doesn't listen. She refuses. They have to be people who'll come and help them. They'll put the evil man away and finally take them home where they'll be safe with their families. She waves and shouts. Her voice is dying as the vans come to a stop before the house, shining their bright lights on the two girls. They're so bright they have to raise their hands to shield their eyes.

The doors to the vehicles open. No shouts of "police!" As the headlights die down, the girls blink, catching sight of several Hispanic men with dark hair and wearing black dress shoes and suits. They look like they're heading to a business meeting or a funeral. The girls stare at each other, their hearts sinking.

The nearest walks towards them with a slight frown on his face. He's clutching a cigar, the end flaring orange as he takes a drag, his mouth twisting into a mocking smile.

"Hello, girls," he says, flicking ash onto the dry grass at their feet. "Are you ready to take a little ride?"

#

Mercari heads towards her friends at their lockers the next morning, so excited she can barely stop herself from running.

"You guys have to see what I've got!" she says.

"What?" asks Kathy. Jane is with them today, her strawberry blonde hair in a braid down her back.

"I bet you can't wait," Mercari teases, digging into her bag.

"Oh gosh, tell us already!" says Jane, clutching her textbook to her chest. The hallway is filled with kids chattering and opening and closing their lockers with loud bangs, teasing and laughing as teachers file between them, trying to make their way to their classrooms in the chaos.

Mercari pulls her cell phone from her bag, and the girls shriek with joy.

"I can't believe your mom finally gave in!" says

Shelly, admiring the brand-new phone. "That's a pretty good model, too."

"It was actually my dad who pushed the issue," says Mercari, her dark eyes shining as she beams at her friends.

"Brownie points for Dad," remarks Jane, snatching the phone from Mercari's fingers and taking a closer look. "You have to join our chat group."

"Yeah, that's where we post everything that's going on," says Shelly as Jane hands the phone back.

"Count me in," says Mercari, excited. Finally, she's not the only uncool kid without a phone anymore! She can chat to her friends any time of the day or night, keep up with what's happening, and share silly photos…

The school bell rings, and there's a hustle and bustle around them as the kids head to their class. "Download that app," Jane shouts over her shoulder. "We'll add you to the chat later."

"I will! Talk to you guys later!"

\#

After school that day, Mercari is home alone as her

grandmother left to go to the store. Taking advantage of the situation, she's rummaging in the refrigerator for stuff to make a sandwich. Her phone lights up with a new message, so after dumping the lunch meat, lettuce, and mayonnaise on the counter, she snatches it up.

The message is from an unknown number. *What are you doing?*

Who is this? Mercari texts back. Not many people have her number yet.

Are you home? Another message pops up.

She's about to reply when her phone starts ringing. "Hello?"

"Hey, Cari! What are you up to?" says Jane.

"Nothing too much," says Mercari, frowning. "You okay?" Her friend's voice sounds weird, like she's been crying.

There's silence for a second. "Yeah, I'm fine. I think I have a cold," she gives a loud sniffle. "What are you up to?"

"Just making a sandwich and chill, I guess." She feels so cool with her phone, chatting to her friend from home.

"Do you want to go get some ice cream?"

Mercari's mouth waters. "Well, my grandma's watching me, but she stepped outside for a sec." Her mom would die if she knew her grandma had left her alone in the house for even a moment. "She would freak," Mercari laughs, balancing the phone between her ear and her hunched shoulder as she spreads mayonnaise on her bread. "I'll ask my grandma when she gets back. She shouldn't be long."

As she speaks, the doorbell rings.

"Gotta go, Jane. Someone's at the door. Later."

Leaving her phone beside her half-made sandwich, Mercari heads to the front door. It's Shelby.

"Hey, Mercari," she has her hands behind her back, rocking back and forth. "Oh, uh… is your mom here?" she glances past the little girl and into the house.

"Not right now," Mercari says. "She's on that business trip."

Shouldn't she know that?

"Aww, I guess she left already, huh?" her weird, sad tone

makes Mercari frown.

"Yeah, she did."

"Are you here all by yourself?"

"Not anymore," Mercari points over the woman's shoulder to where a car is pulling up at the driveway. "That's my grandma."

Shelby looks back at Mercari with a small smile. "Well, I better run. See you later." She pulls Mercari into a hug and waves goodbye.

#

Later that night, Mercari's room is lit up with a lamp on the bedside table and some sparkly fairy lights her father gave her after Christmas last year. They give off a comforting glow in the darkness. Mercari's listening to music with headphones on her new phone, loving all the things her new device can do. She has a magazine in her hands, flipping through the pages.

Her phone buzzes, interrupting the music.

Hey, where are you? You missed all the fun at the ice

cream parlor!

Mercari swallows; she forgot about getting ice cream with Jane. She texts back, *my grandma came back sooner than expected. It was hard to get away. Sorry.*

Another message pops up seconds after she's sent it. *Why don't you come meet us right now? Have some fun under the stars!*

Mercari glances at the window. She moves the curtain aside slightly, checking outside. The wind has died down. A car comes up the road, beaming its bright headlights as it passes. She jumps back into bed and types, *It's really dark. Do your parents know y'all are out?*

Jane sends a laughing emoji, and a message appears beneath it. *That's what makes it so special, Cari. We'll be back home before anyone notices. Are you in or not?*

Mercari's heart aches at the thought of her girlfriends hanging out without her. Isn't this part of the reason she wanted a cell phone, so she could keep up with her friends?

She hesitates, glancing over at a nearby chair where her denim jacket and shoes sit in the corner, almost as if they're waiting for her. She glances back at the phone in her hand, then slowly texts, *Alright. I'll be there, but I can't stay long.*

Atta girl!

Heartened by her friend's praise, Mercari slips out of bed and gets dressed, careful not to make too much noise. She snatches the denim jacket from her chair and pulls it on, glancing at her mirror to quickly fix her hair, which is now long and straight. Her heart is pounding with excitement. She's sneaking out to see her friends! She's never done this before. It feels grown-up and mischievous. She grins at her reflection.

As she grabs her phone, she bumps into her bedside table, knocking off a framed photo of her and her mom. She bends down to pick it up, gazing at the picture for a moment. It's a couple of years old, Mercari laughing as Jasmine carries her on her shoulders. She places it neatly on the stand and opens her bedroom door with a low creak.

Her grandmother always sleeps early and has already retired for the night. The hallway light is on, and Mercari looks up and down the upstairs corridor before stepping out, nerves tingling through her. If her mother knew she was sneaking out, she'd go crazy.

Her grandma is in the guest room, her door wide open. The lamp beside her is still on, and there's a book on her chest, a flower print comforter over her body, and glasses on top of her head. She's asleep, one arm hanging off the bed as her mouth is wide open in a soft snore.

Mercari approaches the room. She has to pass it to reach the stairs. Her heart thrums nervously. If her grandma sees her dressed and with her backpack, she'll know she's trying to sneak out.

As she reaches the door, her grandma lets out a loud cough, making Mercari freeze in her tracks.

She turns over in bed, and the book falls to the carpeted floor. Mercari lets out a silent breath of relief and creeps down the stairs, avoiding the ones she knows will creak.

A thrill of excitement jolts through her. *I'm sneaking out!*

She tiptoes over to the living room and resets the alarm to the house. Then she pushes the door open into the late fall night. She shivers slightly as the icy air blows her hair back and pulls on her jacket.

A little nervous, she pulls out her earbuds and plugs them into her phone. There isn't a soul in sight, not even a car driving by. Her neighbors' houses aren't even lit, though the streetlamps light Mercari's way as her favorite music plays in her ears. It feels so weird being out at night by herself. She makes her way down the road and makes a left turn.

Hey! You almost here?

She's looking at the bright screen on her phone as she crosses the street, not looking where she's going. Bright lights suddenly glare at her, and she screams as a car comes at her full speed, screeching to a halt just a few inches away. Mercari stands there like a frightened deer, eyes wide, her breathing coming fast and hard.

"Hey, watch where you're going!" shouts a guy, leaning out of his window. "I almost ran you over!"

"S-sorry," Mercari whimpers.

"There's no reason for a child to be out this late at night anyhow," the man grumbles. He shakes his fist at her as she scurries onto the sidewalk, her legs shaking so much she can barely make it. The car speeds off, beeping his horn as she stands clutching her chest. *That was close.*

She'll have to be more careful.

She watches until the vehicle turns a corner and disappears. Then she glances towards the park. It's dark in there, with few street lamps, the trees whispering in the cold wind. Still shivering, partly from cold and partly from shock, Mercari rips out her earbuds and texts Jane, *I'm here. I don't see you guys anywhere.*

It's a large park, a place where Mercari came a lot with her parents when she was younger. Several wooden benches surround a pond which, in the daytime, has ducks swimming around the reeds. The trees bloom in the spring, attracting photographers from all over. Now, however, the trees are frightening and skeletal. Something nearby, maybe some trash, blows along the grass.

"Where are you guys?" Mercari whispers.

"Here I am," says a small voice.

Mercari whirls around to see a girl her age standing by a nearby tree, waving. Mercari squints. "Is that you, Jane?"

"Yes, it's me."

There's something wrong. Jane is alone and shivering, and as she steps into the streetlamp light, Mercari sees her tangled blonde hair matted with dirt. She's only wearing a white top, torn at the shoulder, jean shorts that have seen better days, and she steps gingerly towards Mercari with bare feet. Cold fear splashes like ice water down the girl's back.

"Jane, what's going on?"

Several leaves stick to the girl's dirty shirt as though she's been rolling around on the ground. She shakes from the cold, tears falling down her dirty face. Silence takes over as the cold wind ripples their clothes. Mercari stares at her friend in shock.

"Oh my God," says Mercari, finally finding her voice. "What happened to you?"

She hugs her tightly as Jane trembles against her, shoulders shaking from fears.

"What happened? You're freezing!"

Jane's cries become wails like she's terrified.

"Say something!" Mercari's truly scared now. She shakes Jane's shoulders. "Tell me what happened!"

Jane sniffles. "You know I'd never put you in harm's way. I love you so much."

"What are you talking about?"

"It wasn't me that texted you," Jane cries, wiping her eyes. "I'm sorry, Mercari. They made me."

"You're scaring me," says Mercari as Jane steps back. "Let's go home."

Jane shakes her head, pointing a trembling finger behind Mercari. She slowly turns around to see a stranger wearing a black suit and a white tie, a dark mask over their face. Mercari swallows, taking a step back as the man tilts his head. She can't see his mouth, but she can tell he's smiling.

"Hey, Mercari. Glad you could join us. You couldn't have

come at a better time."

"Let's go!" Mercari yells, grabbing Jane's hand as the man laughs behind them. Jane, still sobbing, runs through the park and towards the path that leads around the pond.

"Help!" Mercari screams as they stagger along, Jane's bare feet slapping the stone. "Help us!"

The cold fear is like a knife in Mercari's chest. She glances back to see how far they've come, and they gasp and skid to a halt as another man appears from behind a nearby tree, holding a stick in his hand.

Pain explodes in Mercari's head as he swings it, knocking her to the ground. Her cell phone rolls away, stopping just short of the water. Jane collapses beside her, and both girls groan. Bright stars blink in Mercari's vision as pain erupts in her skull.

"Going somewhere, girls?" says a woman's voice. The silhouette of a woman stands above them, hands on her hips as Mercari faints.

#

A black mini-SUV rounds the corner into the driveway. Jasmine rubs her eyes. What a waste of time that supposed "business trip" that was only a few hours away.

She gets inside and rubs her sore feet, looking forward to a hot drink and bed. She makes her way inside, sliding off her heels and wincing as she holds her sore ankle. All is quiet in the house.

She heads upstairs and cracks open Mercari's door.

The bed's empty.

Blinking, Jasmine marches in and pulls aside the bedcovers. Mercari's not there. *The bathroom, maybe?*

To her relief, she hears the toilet flush, but it's Mercari's grandmother heading out. She rubs her eyes. "Jasmine, you're back," she says in surprise.

"Where's Mercari?"

"She's in bed," her mother frowns. "I just checked on her before."

"When before?" fear spills cold on Jasmine. "Mercari? Mercari!"

She runs around the whole house, her breath coming quickly,

terror gripping her. She's not in the living room. Nor the kitchen. Not even the garage or the backyard.

"She's gone!" Jasmine cries. This isn't a false alarm, not this time. Mercari would never keep her waiting for this long. She screams until her throat is hoarse, checking every corner, even under the beds and in the closets.

"Mom, they took my child!" Jasmine screams in Mercari's room, sinking to her knees. "They have her!"

Her mother kneels beside her. "No one broke in," she whispers. "Oh, my goodness, my child, I'm so sorry."

Jasmine snatches a nearby teddy bear, one of Mercari's, sobbing as she cuddles it close. She looks up at her mother. "I have to find my baby. They have my baby!" She would never just leave the house.

She's known it for a while. That man who broke into their home; wasn't random. Now Mercari is gone. Jasmine has never felt such primal, ugly fear. It's like a dark monster in her chest, roaring in triumph as it eats away at her.

"I'll call the police," says her mother, getting to her

feet. Jasmine gets up too and runs for the stairs.

"Where are you going?"

"Trust me on this," says Jasmine, heading for the door. She pulls on her sneakers, not bothering with socks.

"Jasmine, are you sure you can do this?" asks her mother, hurrying down the stairs after her.

"Momma, trust me," Jasmine insists as she pulls on her jacket. The wind roars outside in the darkness. *How could Mercari have gone off alone? Her jacket and shoes aren't in her room! Oh God, my baby!*

Her mother takes her wrist, and their eyes meet.

"Mom, let me go. I don't have a choice."

"Then let me come with you," her mother looks at her beseechingly, her gray hair in rollers, standing in her white nightgown.

"It's best that you wait here, in case…" she swallows. "In case she comes home. Call the police. I have to go." She pulls her into a quick hug before fleeing to her car. She tries to breathe slow and steady, but it's impossible. The engine roars to life, flooding the front yard with the beam of her headlights. Jasmine hopes she'll somehow see Mercari there, standing behind a tree or by the road, but there's no one.

#

"Hello? Police, please," says Jasmine's mother, her hands shaking as guilt floods her. It was up to her to take care of Mercari. She had no idea she's gone. Didn't she check on the girl before going to bed?

"What's your emergency?" says the calm voice on the line.

"My… my grandbaby is missing!" a tear dribbles down the woman's dark cheek.

#

Jasmine's driving at breakneck speed, clutching the steering wheel so hard her knuckles have paled to tan. She reaches for her purse and snatches out her phone, finding Kel's number.

"Damn it!" she growls as the phone slides onto the floor. She reaches down for it, her hand scrabbling. As she draws up with the phone in hand, a car blares its horn ahead; she's on the wrong side of the road.

She screams and swerves, missing the other car by inches as tires screech. Breathing hard, Jasmine puts the device on speakerphone, balancing it on her lap, her heart thundering at a thousand miles an hour. She prays he's awake.

"Hello?" says Kel's sleepy voice. "Jasmine?"

"Kel!" Jasmine's voice is full of panic. "They took our child!"

"Jas? What are you saying?"

"Mercari's missing!"

There's silence, then Kel's voice comes out in a growl. "I'll kill anyone who touches a hair on her head."

"Kel, you have to come out and meet me. I know where she is and who's got her." I have no clue where to look, but I'll drive down highway 57 since many people from out of town take that route.

#

Mercari's never been so scared.

Dull agony pounds in her skull, the darkness around her oppressive. A thick piece of tape is over her mouth, and ropes are tied around her wrists and ankles. She and Jane were bundled into a white van twenty minutes earlier, and now it rumbles along the street, Mercari with no idea where she is or where they're going. Panic has her in its icy grip, and her chest heaves with her rapid breathing.

Her eyes land on the nearby man in black, the mask still over his face and a gun in his hand. He smiles at her, pulling off his mask, and a cold realization dawns on her as she recognizes his features. She breaks into sobs, the sound muffled by the tape, hot tears dribbling down her cheeks. *No, no, no! Why?*

The man peels off one of his gloves and reaches over to caress Mercari's hair. She recoils from him, her stomach squirming. Jane moans beside her, her eyelids flickering. There's blood on her blonde hair from where she was hit.

"Aww, girls, please don't cry," says the man. "I won't hurt you, I promise. I can't speak for the ones you'll be sold to, though." He gives a wicked grin.

Mercari grunts, turning her head and trying to get as far from the kidnapper as possible. The man chuckles, then lays a finger over his lips, telling them to hush. Mercari sniffles, fear turning to panic.

The guy's cellphone rings. Over the rumbling of the van's engine, Mercari can hear the voice on the other line.

"How far are you?"

"Not too far away," says the man, his cold eyes regarding the girls on the floor of the van.

"You got some girls?"

Mercari moans in terror. These are the men kidnapping all the girls across town. The girls who are never seen again. Horror beats feverish in her heart.

I'll never see Mom or Dad again.

"Yes, I do. I think you'll be pleased with them."

Mercari hears the man chuckle. "I hope so. You don't want to disappoint me." There's a strange noise in the background, almost like a muffled yell; a man's. "You know what I do when I get disappointed."

"I won't, sir. That's a promise."

Jane stirs beside Mercari, coming to consciousness. Her eyes are wide as she glances around the van, then at Mercari. She tries to scream, but it's muffled against the tape.

"There's a mess I need to clean up," says the deep voice on the line. "I'll be expecting you soon. We're running out of time."

"Yes, sir."

The man hangs up the phone and thumps on the wall separating the small room from the driver. "Step on it. They're onto us."

#

The man in the basement hangs up the phone, glancing at the two shivering men tied up on the floor nearby, wearing identical black jackets. A single dusty lightbulb shines above their heads, casting meager light in the dim room. Both men are gagged, breathing hard through their noses as they stare up at their captor.

He walks back and forth in front of them, heavy boots thudding. "You had one assignment," he rumbles. "To get girls. Strip them to their underwear, take a video for the buyers, and get the bids started. But you failed."

He scratches his eyebrow with a sigh. "Tell me this is a dream!" he bellows at them.

The nearest man gives a squeal of fright, muffled from the tape on his mouth.

"I think Rick has something to say," says a fourth man, who is watching from the back. He's the Boss, a powerful figure with a voice and demeanor that demands respect.

The man roughly rips off the tape from Rick's mouth. He gasps, breathing in ragged sobs. "I swear! I swear we were trying to get you the best girls! But they escaped!" he cried. He is an ugly guy with a scar on his temple and an unkempt beard verging somewhere between ginger and brown.

"So, you starve them? Beat them? Make them sleep on concrete?" the man roars. "We lose money that way! You lie to me, and you know what happens to liars!"

Rick shakes his head, crying, dribbling tears onto the floor. "It's not what you think, I swear. You got it all wrong."

The man beside him nods vigorously in agreement.

"Look at this," snarls their captor, pulling a newspaper from his jacket and handing it to the Boss. He looks out of place in this shabby basement, wearing a clean suit. His face is clean-shaven. He gets in front of the tied-up men, balancing on the balls of his feet as his knees bend. He holds up the newspaper.

"You see these girls are missing," he says, his voice a low rumble. "Yet we don't have them."

Silence descends in the basement. The Boss slaps the nearest man with the newspaper. "Now you know what's about to happen to idiots who can't follow simple directions. See, they're dealt with." He rises to his feet. "We've got to make a move. They're closing in on us."

Not sparing another glance for the cowering men on the floor, he pulls out a cellphone and jabs the screen as he makes his way up the basement stairs, shoes thumping. As the door closes behind him, a pained shriek echoes around the basement.

Before he's taken three steps, two gunshots ring beneath his feet.

#

Mercari's heart hammers against her ribcage as the van speeds along. She has no idea where she is. Jane hyperventilates beside her, and they both recoil when the man approaches. The gun is gone, but now he's holding a knife. Mercari freezes in horror as the blade slashes, cutting through Jane's shirt and exposing her white bra. They both scream, but the tape muffles their cries of terror.

He stares at Jane's bare stomach and bra for a moment as anger ripples through Mercari. How dare he humiliate her friend like this? She tries to wriggle in the ropes, but she can't move. Jane's chest heaves beside her as she stares wide-eyed at their captor.

He pulls off her shorts as she cries through the tape, fresh tears sliding down her cheeks as she trembles in her underwear. Then he flattens her hair. "Perfect," the man leers and snaps a photo.

She turns her head away, nudging Mercari's shoulder with her forehead as she sobs and Mercari's heart bleeds.

The man kneels and roughly pulls the tape from Jane's mouth. She coughs and says, "What are you doing?"

Ignoring her, he steps back for another photo. She turns her head as the camera flashes, and he kneels to slap her hard across the cheek. Jane gasps, breathing hard, her pale cheek going red. She sobs.

"What's going on back there?" says the driver's voice.

"Shut up and drive!" their captor snarls. "That's your only job. Get us there in one piece; I'm handling this." He looks down at Jane and takes her chin in his fingers, gently tilting her head so she's facing him. Her lip trembles. "Now, let me take a nice picture of you, or the worst will happen. Do you understand me, little girl?"

Sniffling, Jane nods.

"Good," he straightens. "Now fix your face. How about a smile?"

Mercari's soul screams in rage and fright as Jane forces her lips into a smile, even as her body trembles and her eyes glisten with tears.

"That's a good girl," the guy says, snapping more pictures. Then he takes the tape and presses it back over Jane's mouth.

He takes the tape off Mercari's mouth next. She can feel the sticky residue on her skin and lips. "Why?" she whimpers. "Why are you being so evil? I thought you loved my mom."

"We don't have time for dramas now," the man rolls his eyes. "I have a job to do. Damn, I really do love your mom, though. Good point."

The sarcasm drips from his words, making Mercari angry and terrified at the same time. She squirms as the man starts unbuttoning her pants. "I need to use the restroom."

He sighs, glaring at her.

"Jane needs to go too," she says, her eyes sliding to her friend, who gives a vigorous nod. "Can we stop at the side of the road, please? I can't hold it."

"There's no time for that," says the man, unbuttoning her

jeans.

"Please stop the car!" Mercari bellows to the driver.

"What?" the driver's voice comes back.

"Didn't I tell you to mind your damn business?" growls the captor. "Keep your eyes on the road!"

The van suddenly lurches as the driver yells. Bright headlights pour into the van as it collides with an oncoming car. Steel splinters and crashes, and there's a roar, a terrible sound of shattering glass. The van rolls over, throwing everyone inside around before it crashes to a halt.

Silent descends. The driver sits slumped, bleeding from his head. A man and the young girls lie unconscious, bleeding and unmoving.

#

"Jas, how far are you from the area?" I'm on highway 57 by the small wooden Winston Store.

"I'm about fifteen minutes away, Kel." Tears dribble down her cheeks. "Oh, God."

"Stay strong, sweetheart. We'll find her. I know it's

hard, but try to stay positive. She's counting on us."

"I can't lose my baby!" Jasmine cries, wiping at her eyes as she clutches the steering wheel with her free hand.

"We have to focus. You're an amazing mom, always have been. You've never let her down, and you won't now. Do you hear me?"

"I hear you, Kel."

The phone slips from her lap and onto the floor. Taking a deep breath, Jasmine steps on the accelerator.

#

Mercari slowly opens her eyes, confusion and pain rippling through her. Everything hurts. She blinks until her eyes are in focus, groaning. Rain is falling, plinking on the ruined van that now lies on its side. The coppery scent of blood fills her nose.

"Somebody… help me," she whispers.

Feelings slowly come back to her legs, but she's bruised all over. She can feel the burning pain of cuts on her skin, her head pounding with pain. The light of a street lamp illuminates the road outside, and she shivers in fright.

Someone moves near her. "Hello?"

She lifts her head; it feels as heavy as a building.

"I need help," she says. "I... don't know if I can move."

No one responds. Mercari tries to bend her legs. They prickle, but they seem to be all right. *I need to untie myself.*

Her wrists are still tied before her with rope. She wriggles over to the broken window, where shards of glass are still stuck at the edges. She finds a sharp piece and rubs the rope against it, teeth clenched, trying to cut through her bonds.

Her eye catches something outside. Among the falling rain, there's a dark shape by a tree. Her heart clenches; it's a man, slumped. He flew right out of the van.

She gives a scared moan as his eyes flicker open, and he frowns, looking around, confused as to why he's wet. He rolls himself up and leans on the tree for support, his jacket rapidly getting drenched.

Mercari moves faster, slicing the glass through the

ropes, her breath coming in ragged, scared gasps. The man has an injured leg; she can see it from here, and he limps slowly towards the van, his face contorted in pain.

"Mercari!" yells the man. Nothing but the falling rain answers him.

Mercari finally cuts through the bonds and backs away from the sharp glass, rubbing her wrists. She can feel cuts and bruises on her, but it's too dark to see anything inside the van. She can't even see Jane.

"I just want to go home," she cries. Her head tilts, and she sees a dark shape, chest slowly moving up and down.

"A person?" Mercari crawls over. The roof of the van, or perhaps it's the side, it's difficult to tell in the darkness, has crumpled like a soda can, trapping the person inside. The person lies there, the mask still covering their face, giving a weak moan.

Mercari slowly pulls the mask off their face, her heart seizing as she recognizes the blonde hair, the pale, pointed features.

"Shelby?"

Shelby's eyes flicker, and she lets out a pained moan, almost a scream. Taylor limps faster towards the van.

"Mercari!"

"Oh, Shelby, no," Mercari's eyes burn. Shelby shudders and lies still, her eyes open and unseeing.

Sniffling, she closes Shelby's eyes. She can't stay here. They both betrayed her mother, kidnapped her and Jane. She can't even see Jane in here. She needs to escape.

Mercari crawls towards the window, pulling herself along on her elbows. Taylor is gone. Breath becoming frantic, Mercari squeezes herself through the window. She suddenly cries out in pain as glass slices through her palm. She holds it up; a gash has appeared in her hand, bleeding freely. She clenches her teeth through the burning agony, her tears mingling with the rain.

#

Digging a grave in the rain is no picnic.

The men would be sweating if it weren't for the downpour that suddenly assaulted them. The mud is thick and heavy, and it takes longer than usual to dig two shallow graves, where they throw the men's bodies before scooping up more of the thick sludge.

The Boss appears at the doorway, pulling on a black glove, an umbrella over his head. "You done? We need to make a move. Something's wrong. Grab the others, and let's go."

They force the malnourished, sniffling girls out of the house, wrists bound with chains, their knotted hair getting drenched in the rain as they shiver in their torn clothes. They bundle them into the waiting black vans, and the headlights glare through the rainy darkness, the vans rumbling along the long dirt road.

#

Taylor limps towards the van. "Shelby!"

He bends over, clutching his injured leg, teeth bared. He leans into the ruined vehicle.

"There you are," He mutters, reaching to tap Shelby's shoulder. "Shelby, honey, look at me."

He leans into the van and gives a sharp gasp as he tilts Shelby's head. He retches, bile burning his mouth as he throws up outside. *Sweet Jesus. She's dead.*

#

Mercari stumbles into a nearby group of trees, sobbing as she clutches her injured hand. Rain drums on her head, soaking her to the bone. She glances behind and sees Taylor getting to his feet, and she tries to run, pain slicing through her legs. She suddenly trips over something and falls face-first in the wet mud, groaning.

It's a body. Her stomach lurches as she examines it.

"Oh, God! Jane!"

Her friend's lifeless form is lying in the grass. Was it thrown out of the van when they crashed? Mercari clutches her friend, sobbing. Why, why did she come out tonight? She should be at home, safe in bed. Instead, everything her mom warned her about has come true.

"Jane, I'm sorry," she weeps.

Nearby, Taylor pulls out his gun.

#

Jasmine spots the overturned van nearby and slams on the brakes, fear rippling through her. She's about to call an ambulance when she sees a limping figure, a streetlamp casting its orange glow through the line to reveal a gun in his hand.

Heart hammering, Jasmine stops the car and gets out.

#

"There you are," Taylor growls through his teeth as he approaches Mercari. The little girl stares up at him, numb from shock and fear. Then she gets to her feet, her knees shaking, her heart screaming at her to run.

"Don't move!" he snaps and points the gun at her.

"No, Mercari! Get down!" cries a woman.

Mercari's heart lifts. *Mom?*

Taylor swivels around and fires his gun.

#

Hearing the explosive ring of a gunshot makes Jasmine dive behind the nearest tree, her heart pounding in fear against her ribs. It missed her, though the bullet has chipped the tree. She recognizes that voice, and the betrayal breaks her heart. But she can't lose herself now. That's Mercari out there. She won't save her daughter by falling apart.

"Nice to see you finally joined the party, Jas," Taylor calls.

Anger runs through her, red hot. She let this monster into her house! Instead of hurling insults, she calms herself and calls, "Taylor, you don't have to do this." The tree is hard against her back, the only wall between her and death. "You haven't done anything wrong. Please," she closes her eyes, tears threatening to fall. The rain pounds on her face, ice-cold like tiny hammers on her cheeks. "She's my baby, my only child. Let her go, please, and I promise I won't say a word. It'll be like it never happened."

Only the thundering of the rain greets her. Thunder rumbles on the horizon. "Taylor? Are you still there?"

"Jas, this is something you'll never understand," his voice sounds closer now.

"I do understand," she begs.

"You don't have a clue of what's going on, do you? I joined this group. I didn't know anything about human trafficking. I knew once I was in that it was wrong, but I know too much. There's no way out," he inhales sharply through his teeth like he's in pain. "There's no way out for me. I either do what they say, or they'll kill me!"

"It doesn't have to be like that," Jasmine shouts back, her mind racing. "There's help out there. They can protect the girls. Protect you."

#

Kel's tried ringing Jasmine several more times, but it keeps going to voicemail. He turns a corner and sees her car abandoned on the road. Confused, his gaze slides over to the other side of the street, where a van sits on its side in the rain, half of it crumpled like another vehicle hit it.

He leaves his engine running and climbs out of his car, the torrential rain pouring on him and soaking him in seconds. It's dark, but he spots a tree nearby, a figure bent before it as if he's injured.

"…you still there?" Jasmine's voice floats towards him.

#

Jasmine takes a steeling breath and slowly emerges from behind the tree, her hands up. What do negotiators do? They form a bond of trust between them and the criminal. She and Taylor have dated; she let him kiss her. More! There has to be some affection in his heart for her, surely?

Taylor is holding the gun in her direction, blood pouring from a cut on his head, mingling with the rain falling on his dark hair. Tears burn Jasmine's eyes as she presses her lips together, shaking her head. Has he killed before?

"I'm sorry, Jasmine," he says, finger squeezing the trigger.

"NO!"

Kel runs towards them, shoes squishing in the grass. Taylor turns, and there's an explosive bang; Kel crumples to the ground.

"NO!" Jasmine screams.

Kel grunts on the ground, clutching his stomach. "Run, Jas!"

Sobbing, Jasmine runs for the trees as more gunshots fire behind her. Kel is lying on the wet ground, a pistol in his hand. *Oh God, Kel. Be careful.*

"Mercari!" she cries, slipping between some trees. "Where are you?"

She hears a noise up ahead and wipes her wet face, trying to see in the darkness. Rain pelts the trees, splashing cold water on her as she picks her way along the mud and twigs.

#

Mercari clutches her aching ribs, clenching the fist of her injured hand. She's come to a field on the other side of the trees, the wind blowing the grass before her, several streetlamps illuminating the road.

Her heart lifts as the sound of an engine pierces the rain-filled night. Hoping it's a family or even an ambulance, she stumbles into the road as she waves. Headlights land on her, almost blinding her, as two vans squeal to a stop right before her. Mercari wants to sob with relief.

Men clamber out of the van dressed in black suits. She can hardly see them in the darkness, but their slow gait makes her uneasy. She backs away, suddenly wishing she didn't stop them.

"Hey, sweetie, are you lost?"

Cold fear running through her, Mercari shakes her head, lips pressed together as the rain sticks her hair to her forehead, running in cold rivulets down her skin. Panic makes her lungs constrict, and she struggles to breathe.

"Who… are… you?" she asks, her words coming out weak.

The nearest man pulls on a pair of gloves. He's wearing a suit, dark hair tied behind him. She doesn't like the grin that spreads across his face. "Who I am isn't as important as to why a girl your age would be wandering around all alone in the middle of the night."

He looks over and around her, right over to the trees on the other side of the road as Mercari's heart sinks. *No, no! More bad guys? Why me?*

"Come with us. You shouldn't be out here alone."

Mercari shakes her head, legs trembling as she backs off onto the sidewalk.

"I won't hurt you, I promise." He reaches inside his coat.

"LEAVE MY CHILD ALONE, YOU MONSTER!"

Mercari turns in disbelief to see Jasmine running towards them from the tree line. Her hair is a mess, terror on her face. "Mom?" says Mercari in disbelief.

"Your mother shouldn't let you wander off on your own," says the man. "Anything could happen."

"Mercari, run!"

The little girl turns and flees towards her mother, her heart screaming, fingers outstretched.

"Grab her!" growls the man, and terror floods Mercari as heavy footsteps sound behind her, following her along the road and onto the grass. She screams as strong arms wrap around her waist.

"No!" Jasmine cries. She's still far away. She pelts at full speed towards them, the heavy rain thundering around them, Mercari digging her heels into the grass and shrieking as she reaches towards her mother, the men dragging her towards their van. An enormous guy lifts her over his shoulder, and they sprint back to the vans.

"MOM!" Mercari screams, punching the man's back with

weak fists.

"Let's make a move for it! Now!"

#

"Jasmine!" Kel shouts, running through the forest. The rain is a cacophony of noise around him, and he's dizzied from the pain in his stomach. He can barely walk. He clutches his abdomen, not caring how badly he might be hurt. Ignoring the burning pain and the blackness threatening to overtake his vision, Kel follows the screaming voices ahead.

#

"No! Please, please, no!" Jasmine screams as they drive off in a loud roar of engines. Jasmine collapses to her knees on the roadside, screaming until her throat tears, tears mingling with the relentless rain.

Warm arms wrapped around her, and at first, she resists, sobbing into the dirt. Kel grunts in pain as he pulls her to her feet, hugging her close. "Shh, Jas. It's alright. It's okay."

"No, it's not!" she cries. "She's gone!"

"We'll get her back, I swear. I promise with every fiber of my being. We'll get her back. Trust me."

#

It's after midnight. Jasmine stirs in her sleep, jerking awake and wiping the drool away from her mouth. Outside, descending on her ears as she drifts from unconsciousness, are the sounds of beeping monitors and talking hospital staff.

Nearby, lying in a bed, is Kel, his bandages wrapped around his torso. Despair settles on Jasmine's shoulders like a heavyweight. Despite everything, they still took Mercari. She was within grasp, and they snatched her poor baby away. What awful things is she going through right now? Jasmine can't bear to think about it.

Kel is asleep, his breathing even. *How can he sleep when Mercari is missing?* But he's exhausted; she understands that.

She gets up and pushes the window's curtains aside, looking outside at the sky. The rain stopped shortly after the ambulance brought them here, and now the clouds have parted, the stars twinkling above. The highway is below, and despite the late hour, the occasional car drives past. Fury rushes through her. Of all the vehicles that could have passed Mercari during her escape, it had to be more of the monsters who preyed upon little girls.

A sob crawls up her throat, and Jasmine slaps a hand over her mouth.

"We're going to get her back."

She jumps, the curtain fluttering as she turns to Kel, who's sitting up in bed, pain etched on his face.

"We may never find her, Kel."

She'll become another one of the nameless girls in the "Missing" section of the newspaper, slowly forgotten while their families never know what happened to them. She can't bear to think about where Mercari might be right now, what that filth is doing to her.

"They have the borders surrounded. They won't get far," says her husband, his voice firm. Is he trying to convince her or himself? "We'll find her, Jas. Trust me."

He takes her hand, his fingers warm.

#

Kel watches Jasmine sleep, glad she's finally getting some rest. The bullet in his abdomen, just an inch from killing him, according to the doctor, will take a while to heal. They kept him here, monitoring them both for shock and other injuries while the authorities chased the men who took Mercari. Kel's been hoping the police will contact him, saying they found her, but he's heard nothing so far.

He has to be strong for his wife. He and Jasmine might be separated, but that doesn't mean he feels nothing for her.

There's a gentle knock on the door, and a Caucasian nurse wearing scrubs and short blonde hair comes in. "Knock, knock," she smiles. "Good morning."

"Morning," says Kel.

"How are you feeling today?"

"Good as new," he says, gesturing to the bandage. Kel will do anything to leave the hospital as fast as possible.

"Well, everything looks good," she says after examining him. "We can release you today if you like. Just make sure to get plenty of rest."

Jasmine stirs at the sound of voices, her eyes slowly opening as she sits up, the sheet a nurse gave her falling off her. "Have we heard anything?" she asks, stretching.

"Nothing," says Kel, and the look on Jasmine's face breaks his heart.

"I hope I didn't wake you," says the nurse.

"No, it's okay. How is he?"

"Pretty good. He's strong; he'll recover in no time. The doctor will make a final check of you both," her blue eyes linger on Kel. "Do you need help getting dressed, Mr. Johnson?"

"I think I got it," he says. "But thanks."

She smiles at him and leaves the room as Jasmine shakes her head. "Unbelievable."

She helps Kel sit up. "I'll get your things."

He watches her as she gets his clothes from a nearby locker, returning with his shirt and jeans. That she quickly picked up from the house to the hospital. When he's sitting at the edge of the bed, she unties his hospital gown and lets the material fall away, exposing his bareback. Her fingers linger on his shoulder for a moment, her touch like feathers.

"You're so beautiful, you know?" says Kel softly, gazing into her eyes. Maybe it's the anguish that has united them, the fragility of everything, but she feels a rush of warmth as his dark brown eyes look at her. He leans in, lips parting.

"Kel, don't," she whispers, heat turning to shame. She helps him put on his shirt. When she's finished, he takes her chin in his hand and gently turns her face to his. Tears burn her eyes.

"I love you, Jas, let me be your strength," he whispers and plants a warm kiss on her lips.

#

A week later, Jasmine is watching the news. A reporter she knows by sight is holding a microphone, her face grim.

"Today marks a week since Mercari Johnson, daughter of our very own Jasmine Johnson, went missing. She was taken in a van against her will and hasn't been seen since."

A picture of Mercari, a school picture from about a year ago, pops up onto the screen. Jasmine stifles a sob, eyes brimming with tears.

"The pandemic of human trafficking is continuing to grow," the pale-skinned reporter's face is contorted in her grief. "Girls continue to go missing with no traces of their whereabouts. The police urge communities to come together during these difficult times. Keep your families safe, and if you have any information, no matter how small or seemingly insignificant, please contact your local authorities."

It's awful to see Mercari on the news. A statistic.

The news switches off, and Kel is there with the remote controller. He wraps his arms around Jasmine and holds her close, making soothing "shh" noises as her shoulders shake.

"Come on, Jas. We have to be strong to get our angel back."

"I know, I know," she cries, wiping her eyes. She's shed so many tears this past week she's surprised she hasn't run out. "I just miss our little girl so much."

"I miss her, too. We'll get her back."

How? It's been a week, and we're no closer to finding her.

Silence takes over until Kel says, "Come on, let's finish putting out signs in case someone's seen her."

It feels good to do something, even if it's pointless. They gather the posters, information about Mercari and her picture. Jasmine's worst nightmare. When she opens the front door, they both blink in astonishment.

"Oh, my poor babies," says an older lady, her iron-gray hair curled, wearing a shawl around her large shoulders. "I just can't believe this is happening." She reaches out her hands, taking Jasmine and Kel's fingers in hers.

"Mom," says Kel, and they both embrace the older woman. She shuffles inside.

"I can't sleep, I can't eat," she sniffles, blowing her nose noisily into a brightly colored handkerchief.

Jasmine can't remember the last time she ate, and what little sleep she can get is overrun by terrible nightmares. "We'll find her," is all she can say. It's like a mantra. If she and Kel keep saying it, it'll come true.

They guide Kel's mother to the couch, and Jasmine runs to make her some tea.

"Listen, Mom. Stay here and rest. I believe that God will bring back our baby," says Kel. "The last thing I need is for my mother to make herself ill. Jas and I are going to go and put out more flyers."

"I won't sit here like a helpless old woman!" says Kel's mother. "She's my grandchild. I won't take no for an answer."

Jasmine comes in with the tea, sharing a look with her husband.

"Okay, Mom, if you're up for it," says Kel, not in the mood to argue. "We won't try to change your mind."

#

In a small town with a tight-knit community, fields surround simple houses. A deep wood lies nearby, old wooden houses and a gurgling river that runs behind them. The river has been used as a dumping ground for decades, and trash lies in the stream. Some of the trees are dead-looking, ruined by the pollution. The setting sun casts red light on the woods in deep slits.

Several girls, varying in ages from twelve to eighteen, are in the river up to their knees, connected by chains clamped around their ankles. Five men stand nearby, flanking the group, black guns in their hands.

Each girl holds a rag, trying their best to clean themselves in the water that flows cold and not so fresh. The guards watch with hard, cold eyes, silently daring any of them to try to run.

Bruises are scattered among most of the girls' malnourished bodies. At the end of the chain link is Mercari, her hair matted with dirt and tied up in a bun.

"Hey," she whispers to a nearby girl. The girl is pale-skinned and blonde, with nasty purple bruises up and down her skinny arms.

"You're not still planning on running away?" the girl murmurs, keeping her head down so the guards don't see her lips moving.

"Yes! I'm not staying here another minute. I miss my mom and dad," Mercari whispers. Since she was snatched and bundled into the van, everything has been a terrible blur of pain and fear. She rinses her legs with water, watching the dirt slide off.

"Don't be stupid," the girl whispers. "You saw what happened to April. They…" she sniffles. "Sliced her throat! Right in front of us!"

Mercari swallows. She looked away when the guards took a dagger to the fourteen-year old's throat, but she would never forget the screams.

"Mercari, they'll kill you, too."

"That's a chance I'll have to take," says Mercari, determination swallowing her fear. What's the point in being alive if they have to live like this?

A hand snatches her by the arm, and she cries out in shock. A tall girl with short black hair, wet from the river, wearing a white shirt and jean shorts, marches her from the river.

"Ouch! You're hurting me," Mercari snarls, trying to pull her arm from the girl's grip.

"Listen, you little brat," the girl says in a forced whisper as a nearby guard watches them. "You'd rather have me tending to you than one of those creeps. Because trust me, you won't know the meaning of hurt until they get a hold of you." She glances at the guards, "Which they will soon. Now," she moves closer to Mercari, then unlocks the padlock around her ankle. "Do as I tell you, or you'll vanish like the other girls. Understand?"

Mercari stares back at the girl. Her dark hair sticks to her pale cheek, a blueish tinge at the corner of the eye like someone has punched her in the face. Mercari says nothing as the heavy footsteps of a guard approach. He's an ugly older man, a cigarette between his lips as he smirks down at them. "Is there a problem over here?"

"No, sir, of course not," says the girl quickly, her grip sliding from Mercari's arm.

The man chuckles, throwing away his cigarette and crushing it beneath his boot. Without warning, he grabs the girl's hair and yanks her to him. Her face screws up in fear and pain, teeth clenched as he holds her so close their faces almost touch.

"You control the munchkin, or I'll take care of you both," he hisses and shoves her away from him. Scowling, the girl pulls Mercari by the arm into a nearby log cabin.

"What's going on?" cries Mercari, her heart pounding in fear as the girl half-drags her into a tiny bathroom with a toilet and a washbasin. A small bathtub sits in the corner.

"Take your clothes off."

"W-what?"

The girl pushes past her and runs water in the bathtub.

"I just took a bath," says Mercari, not moving. "I don't need another one."

The girl sighs, getting to her feet while water gushes into the tub. "Listen, kid. It's about to get real serious. They might not have touched you yet, but it's only because they want to sell you. *Unspoiled*. Do as you're told." She heads towards the door.

"Or what?" asks Mercari. She hates how bossy the girl is, how she's treating everyone like dumb toddlers just because she's a little older.

The teenager rounds on her, staring her down until a

ripple of fear runs through the little girl.

"Or they'll kill me, right?"

"Take a bath as soon as it's ready," the girl mutters, turning away so Mercari can get undressed.

Stripping off, Mercari gets into the tub of lukewarm water. It's better than the filthy river, at least. A wave of despair washes over her, and suddenly, she's crying, missing her parents, hating her situation and the guards, pity stirring in her for herself and the other girls.

#

The girl is about to head outside when she hears voices in a nearby room. She steps close to the door and listens.

"Listen, there's surveillance pretty much everywhere on the whereabouts of this Mercari girl," says a deep voice she recognizes; he's one of the higher-ups who loves to beat the girls when they misbehave. "That overseas buyer won't wait forever. This girl's parents aren't giving up. Her mom is some hotshot Reporter; she's high-profile."

"There isn't much time left," says another voice, higher

pitched. "She's got to be shipped out in the next three days."

"We've got no choice, then. We have to act fast."

#

One of the men, dressed in a black vest and gray pants, takes a drag of his cigar. Something near the foot of the door catches his eye; it looks like a shadow. He gets up and creeps to the door, holding up a finger to keep the other man silent.

He yanks the door open, but no one's there.

He marches down the hallway and to one of the bedrooms, where the dark-haired girl is lying, reading a magazine. He can't remember her name, but he remembers her attitude. Lording it over the other kids just because she's one of the oldest. She doesn't even look up as he steps into the room.

"Did you take care of the munchkin?"

"She's taking a bath," says the girl, turning a page in the magazine.

"You should never leave a kid alone," the man growls.

"Whatever you say, sir."

He snatches the magazine from her fingers and throws it onto the floor. She lets out a cry of pain as he grabs her face to force her to look at him. He longs to bruise that pretty jaw. Her dark eyes meet his, and he sees a flicker of rebellion before she wilts in his grasp. He feels a thrill of satisfaction at her submission.

"If you ever eavesdrop again, I'll kill you with my bare hands, you little rat. Do I make myself clear?"

"Yes, sir," the girl responds, panic in her voice. When he throws her aside, she scrambles from the bed to check on Mercari.

#

She pushes the door open to find an empty tub, brown with dirty water and bath towels strewn on the floor. Cold fear wraps around her heart. "Oh no. Mercari, where are you?"

She peeks outside, where the guards are bringing the other girls back. She rushes to the kitchen door, which is ajar. Mercari is out, running from the cabin, her black hair bouncing as she runs. Cursing, the teen girl slips out, closes the door, and follows her.

#

The cold air is sharp in Mercari's lungs as she runs, pine needles and dry grass stabbing her bare feet, fear screaming in her heart as she runs. When she glances back, the dark-haired girl is nearly upon her, fury in her young face. She cries out as the girl tackles her, and they fall to the grass in a tangle of limbs.

"Get off me!" yells the little girl, slapping out at her. The older girl covers her mouth, pinning her to the ground with fire in her eyes.

"Listen to me, you little brat! I'm trying to help you. We have to help each other if we want to stay alive."

"I'm just a kid," Mercari sobs as the girl's hands gently move from her lips. "Why do you need my help?"

"You've got fight in you, and that's good," says the dark-haired girl. "Together, we can make a good team. But we have to play by *my* rules. Just running doesn't work; they'll kill you if they catch you. If you want to stay alive, you must do as I say. Understand?"

Mercari swallows, nodding.

"Now, I have a plan. Remember, do as I say, and

you'll see your parents again."

"You promise?"

There's a pause. "I promise."

She gets off Mercari, brushing loose grass from her clothes. "Here, let me help you up."

#

"Where are Holley and Mercari? They aren't here."

"What do you mean?" growls the ringleader.

"I looked for them everywhere, sir. They aren't here."

The ringleader stares at the man in silence. "Well, don't just stand there like a jackass," he snaps. "Go out and find them!"

"Yes, sir."

The man steps out to the woods, his gun in his hand as his cold eyes search the tree line. No girl has managed to escape their little community yet, and he isn't about to get outwitted by two stupid little teenagers. He steps towards a bush, where Mercari and Holley are crouching. He doesn't notice the girls as they watch him, their hearts thumping as he stops before them.

A noise behind makes him turn, and when he lumbers off,

Holley gestures for Mercari to follow her.

The guard lets out a gasp of surprise when he turns a corner around the cabin and almost collides with the girls, both holding damp clothes in their arms. "Where've you two been?"

Mercari's face pales as she stares at the ground.

"We came to get the wet clothes," says Holley. "Mercari left them here."

"I looked all over the place and didn't see you," says the guard, his eyes narrowing.

"Well, you didn't look hard enough," Holley shrugs. "We were right there, wringing out the clothes."

He glares at them both until Holley's gaze lowers. "Get inside there now," he snaps.

#

"You ready to go to town? We need toiletries," says a guard to Holley the next day.

"Can Mercari come?"

The guard, Amir, turns to give her an incredulous

look. He's an ugly brute of a thing, with a balding pate and mud-brown eyes. "You know no other girls are allowed in town."

"She could come and try some personal wear," Holley suggests. "She's new; I don't know her size."

The man scratches his stubble-covered chin. "Guess it won't hurt this one time. It ain't like she'll be here much longer anyhow."

The reminder sends a shiver up Holley's spine, but she stands firm.

"Go get her."

She turns to leave, and he snags her shirt. "If either of you tries anything stupid, I'll kill you both myself." He shoves her away from him.

Holley finds Mercari in the bedroom. "He's agreed to let you come."

Nodding, Mercari clambers off the bed as Holley snags up her jacket. "Just remember the plan. We only have one chance. If you mess this up, you'll be shipped off to God knows where." She helps Mercari with her jacket. "Is that understood?"

"Is what understood?"

They both freeze as the guard stands in the doorway.

"I was explaining we have to find her size as quick as we can," says Holley calmly. "Try on some things fast so we can get in and out."

The man smiles, but instead of making him look more pleasant, it somehow makes him scarier. An old scar, like he's taken a blade to the face, stretches white across his cheek. "Great job, Holley. You're the only one of these kids that can be trusted. Let's get going."

#

It's surreal to be rumbling along the road, buildings and cars flitting past like all is well in the world. Mercari shrinks into the jacket around her shoulders, Holley's thin body beside hers in the van. Her heart thumps. Will their plan work?

They stop far away from a large mall's entrance, and the man pulls on a pair of gloves before cutting the van's engine.

"Now, Mercari, here are the rules," he turns to her. "Holley's familiar with them. Keep your jacket hoodie on your head. No looking at people, even if they talk to you. If you use the restroom, don't even think about trying to leave any messages or signs that you're here because I check the stalls myself when you're done."

Mercari shivers beneath his gaze. How many times have girls tried to escape, only for this horrid man to foil their plans?

What chance do we have?

"You got all that, kid?"

"Yes," she says, her voice quiet. They step out of the van and into the cool, fresh air as the man finishes the cigarette in his hand and throws it to the concrete ground.

Mercari glances around at the people in the parking lot. No one gives them a second glance. They push carts full of groceries, buckle their kids into cars, not noticing that two missing girls are feet away.

"Let's go. Stick together," growls Amir, pulling his hood over his head. He snaps his fingers in front of Mercari's face. "Move!"

Mercari yanks her hood over her head, hiding the matted bun

of hair, following Holley and the man to the mall. A woman approaches from ahead, heading to her car. At the last moment, Mercari steps to the side, colliding with the friendly-looking African American lady.

"Oops! Are you okay, sweetie?" she asks. Her voice is so kind Mercari wants to weep.

Holley and the man turn to stare. Thunder is in the man's gaze, silently warning her. Mercari swallows and glances at the woman. "Yes, sorry. I need to watch where I'm going."

"No problem, hon. You all have a good day," the woman smiles and wanders off. As soon as her back's turned, the man grabs Mercari by the elbow and gets down to her level. The stink of cigarette smoke is putrid on her face.

"Pull a move like that again, and you won't have time to be shipped off," he hisses through his yellowing teeth.

He doesn't notice the small nod between the girls. Mercari clutches the stolen cell phone in her pocket.

They venture into the mall. A supermarket is on the first floor, more floors hosting clothes shops and electronics stores. They're silent as they go up an escalator. The clean floors and bright lights are surreal after her prison. Mercari clutches the cell phone in her fist, her heart thumping as her palms sweat.

They go into a clothes store with thumping dance music and pick up some clothes: jeans, shirts, dresses, simple clothes that won't look out of place on a thirteen-year-old. They were heading for the changing rooms when the phone clutched in Mercari's pocket vibrates.

Her heart clenches as she holds the buzzing phone in her hand. Amir looks around, frowning. No one else is around.

"What sizes do you think might be right for you, Mercari?" asks Holley loudly, making as much noise as possible as she shows her the jeans she's picked up. "I don't know. I think these may be a little long for you."

"What's that sound?" the man asks, eyes narrowing. Sweat beads on Mercari's forehead. Their eyes meet for a fraction of a second, and the phone finally stops buzzing. Her shoulders relax.

"Umm, that one," Mercari answers Holley, pointing at a random pair of jeans in the taller girl's arms.

"Hello?" says a nearby woman, holding a cellphone to her ear, pushing a baby buggy with her free hand. There's a pause as they all stare at each other.

"Come on, the dressing room's here," says Holley, taking Mercari by the arm. The man follows so close behind they're almost touching.

"Move fast, you hear me?" he says.

"Of course," Holley calls over her shoulder.

"Same stall," he calls after them. "Keep an eye on her."

To anyone listening, he sounds like a concerned father asking her to take care of a sister. Mercari wants to scream at the people around them, to yell for them to take notice. But he'll kill them both if she does.

"Understood."

Her voice drops once they're inside the stall, and they pull the curtain closed. With trembling fingers, Mercari unlocks the cell phone. Thank God it's not password protected.

"We've got two minutes," Holley whispers so quietly Mercari almost can't hear her. "Hurry, it's our only chance."

Holley pulls down Mercari's pants, making a great show of changing her while Mercari dials her mom's number. Her parents made her memorize it when she was eight, and she's never forgotten it.

#

Jasmine lies on the sofa, Kel's arms around her, eyes sore from crying. She groans as her cell phone rings, wondering if it's the press or the police yet again. She gets up and answers it. The number is unknown.

"Hello?"

"Mom."

Jasmine's heart leaps to her throat. She clutches the phone tight to her ear, fresh tears burning. Could it really be her, or is she dreaming?

"Mercari!"

"Is that her? Is that our girl?" Kel babbles.

"My baby! My God, where are you?" There's pop music playing in the background and a rustle of cloth. It's so good to hear her voice again, but she swallows the thousands of questions wanting to bubble from her lips.

"I don't have much time to talk, Mom. I just want to say that if I don't make it, I love you so much."

Her heart grows cold at that. It sounds like her daughter has already given up. "No, Mercari, tell me where you are."

#

"You girls should be done by now," says Amir as he opens the door to the stall. The girls hold the clothes in their arms, nodding. "Alright, let's go."

When his back's turned, Holley drops a note on the floor behind them.

The girls drag their steps for as long as they can, but soon it's time to leave. As they exit the mall and head across the parking lot, they spot some police cars.

"Don't even think about it," Amir snarls, and the

girls keep their heads down. In the corner of her eye, Mercari sees the African-American lady talking with the police.

#

The staff member rubs her eyes, already tired from her job and still nursing the remnants of a hangover. A phone rings from one of the changing rooms, and she frowns; no one is in there right now.

She pulls aside the curtain and sees a cell phone buzzing on the floor. Someone must have left it here.

Whoever's calling might be able to help me find the owner. "Hello?" She blinks at the panicked voice on the other line. "No, ma'am, they left the dressing room earlier. Yes. Yes, I'll notify the store."

Something else catches her eye; a piece of crumpled paper on the floor. She picks it up and unfurls it.

HELP US is scrawled across the top of the page, and an address is written on it. The staff worker swallows, fear prickling her skin. This is definitely not right.

#

Despair fills Mercari as the car engine rumbles, taking them back to that hellish place. Their plan didn't work. Tears roll down her cheeks as Holley reaches over to give her fingers a comforting squeeze.

#

"Kel, they're an hour away!" Jasmine cries, snatching her keys.

"Let's go."

What a clever girl Mercari is, leaving them an address and using a phone to get in touch. Jasmine just hopes she isn't too late. The police have confiscated the note and the phone. She doesn't want to wait for law enforcement; she needs to see Mercari right now.

#

"Let's go, girls," says Amir as they pull up near the cabin in the woods.

Some more men come to meet him as they clamber out. A big guy with huge shoulders gives Mercari a smirk. "Looks like some of the transactions will be completed ahead of time after all," he says to Amir. "Holley," he snaps. "Get in there and make sure the munchkin is cleaned up."

Cold fear floods Mercari as Holley takes her gently

by the wrist. She doesn't move or make a sound.

Until now, she's kept quiet, managing to keep her panic under control and believing that somehow, she and the other girls would be saved. But it's dawning on her: no one is coming to save them. She, like the girls on the missing posters, will never be found.

"Do you hear Holley talking to you?" Amir snaps, giving her a nudge. "Get going and do as you're told."

Mercari's legs are like jelly as she follows Holley back to the cabin. As soon as the bathroom door is closed, Holley whispers, "Mercari, why didn't you call 911?"

"I had to hear my mom's voice," Mercari whispers, her eyes filling with tears. "I'm sorry." She lets out a dry sob. "I'm going to be shipped out, aren't I?" She still isn't sure what it means, but it can't be anything good.

"No, you're not. Guess what," the older girl takes Mercari's hand in hers.

"What?"

"I dropped a note. I know this place's address. I earned their trust, so I'm allowed to go where I want, within reason. They get letters all the time, and the address is always the same."

Hope dawns in Mercari's heart.

"Someone will come and find us! I know it. And your mom will call the cell back."

Seeing Mercari's sad face, Holley chucks her under the chin. "We can't give up. We need to make a move out of here. The cops might already be on their way."

"But how?"

"I'll distract the guy outside," Holley whispers, her words tumbling from her lips in an excited rush. "Sneak out the side door. There's a big tree there. I'll meet you there, okay?"

"Okay, Holley."

#

Mercari sneaks out of the door, looking both ways before sprinting towards a nearby tree. A guard comes into view, talking on a cell phone, and her heart screams in fear as he glances around. She darts behind the tree, clutching her chest. The guard is silent.

"Yeah, so anyway…" he continues, turning back

around. Mercari breathes as silently as she can, her heart thundering a hundred miles an hour.

Crunching footsteps approach, and she shifts around the tree, silently praying he doesn't see her, edging around the trunk as he walks past. Then he walks off, and she can breathe normally again.

Some men are talking in the distance, smoking and with their guns at their sides.

A hand clamps over her mouth and panic seizes her; she kicks at the ground until Holley whispers in her ear, "Shh! It's me."

The fingers slowly lower from Mercari's lips. "Listen to me. It'll be exactly ten minutes before they notice we're gone. We have to be careful because they set traps, but I believe we can make it to the road."

Already, they can hear the wailing sirens of police in the distance, but this cabin is deep in the woods. They can't rely on law enforcement stumbling across them.

"He's going into the cabin!" Holley whispers, seeing a man going to check on them. "Go!"

They stumble through the bracken and past the trees,

breathing hard as the cold air rushes past their cheeks. Their bodies are thin and weakened, and dry grass and twigs hurt their bare feet, but they don't slow down.

They both duck, terror in their eyes, as a gunshot cracks through the air. Has someone seen them? Staying low, they run through the bushes. Mercari glances back.

Blue lights flash in the tree line, cops getting out of cars and yelling at the men to put their hands above their heads.

Hope dawns…

BANG! More gunshots. The cops duck behind their car doors, guns pointed as the men fire at them. Horror grips Mercari. Will they kill them all?

"Mercari, let's go!" Holley whispers, grabbing Mercari's hand as heavy footsteps follow them. If they're caught now, the men won't hold back; they'd rather kill them than hand them over to the police.

Another gunshot cracks overhead, so close it whistles past Mercari's ear. Heart screaming, blood pumping, the girls run hand in hand until…

"The road!" Holley breathes as they stumble onto a concrete road. Car tires screech and Holley pulls Mercari out of the way of an oncoming car just in time.

"Oh my God! Mercari!" Jasmine gets out of the car, her brown eyes wide as they fall on her daughter. Disbelief is written on her face.

"Mommy!"

It's amazing to be in her mother's arms again, to feel safe for the first time in weeks. Jasmine sobs into her hair, pulling her close. Mercari never wants to let her go.

"I'm so glad you're okay," says her dad, coming to join them and holding them in his arms. For that small moment, Mercari feels safe.

"They're coming! Hurry!" Holley screams. A gunshot cracks through the air, and Mercari watches in horror as Holley's dark eyes widen. She staggers forward for a moment then collapses on the ground.

"Oh no," Mercari whimpers. Holley's shoulder is bleeding.

"Hurry!" Kel snaps, running to the girl and gathering her up in his arms. "Get in the car!"

More gunshots whistle past as men shout in the tree line. Mercari and her family run into the car, Kel depositing Holley on the back seat. The girl's breathing is shallow, red pouring from her shoulder. Jasmine hits the accelerator, and the car takes off down the road.

"Keep your head down, Mercari!" Kel roars as gunshots blast at them. She screams as the back window shatters.

#

Amir aims the gun and shoots again. He grins as a tire bursts and the car veers off the road around the corner. "Come on," he growls at the man beside him, and they run to the vehicle.

His dark eyebrows raise in surprise as he finds the car empty, all the doors open. "What the…?"

He gives a cry as he's suddenly thrown to the ground; Kel has caught up to him, tackling him to the concrete road. The gun skitters away. The pair fight, punching and kicking anywhere they can.

Kel dives for the gun, his fingers wrapping around it as the man delivers a strong punch to his kidney, making him wheeze.

"You'll never take my daughter again!" Kel growls, pointing the gun at Amir.

BANG.

Amir coughs, blood spurting from his thick lips, and he collapses. Kel breathes heavily, regaining his shaking feet, looking around for his family. Jasmine emerges from the tree line, her face drawn. She looks down at the man's dead body in horror.

"Don't move," says another voice as the click of a gun sounds behind her head. Jasmine freezes, slowly raising her hands. She meets Kel's eyes, terror on her face. Kel hides the gun behind his back.

"Where's the girl?"

Jasmine says nothing, tears dribbling down her cheeks as she presses her lips together.

"Cat got your tongue, huh? How about now?"

The gunshot fires before Kel can move, before he can even

gasp. Jasmine crumples to the ground, bleeding from her ear. He grazed her. She clutches her ear, screaming through her teeth.

#

"Mom!" screams Mercari from the trees. Seeing her mother hurt has awakened a new, primal horror in her. The man turns to her, murder in his eyes as he points the gun at the little girl.

BANG.

The man's eyes roll to the back of his head as he crumples to the ground, blood pouring from his skull. Kel stands there, the gun in his shaking hands, breathing hard.

Mercari runs from the trees, pulling along Holley, who's clutching her shoulder. Kel helps up Jasmine. "Are you okay?"

"I think so," she pulls her fingers away from her ear; they're covered in red, and her head's ringing, but she's alive. Kel gathers them all in a hug as they sob.

"It's all over now."

#

A woman in an olive-green dress stands in the woods that was Mercari's prison, talking grimly into a black microphone.

"This is the place where the gang kept the captured girls, where they were brought to be beaten, exchanged and sold, and more," she says, her face drawn. "Many girls from our community were sold overseas or died trying to escape. These events have shaken Grandville to its core. Now, the gang has been shut down, and law enforcement is working on bringing down their associates."

Kel comes in with his arm around Mercari and clicks off the TV. Jasmine rubs her eyes; she just couldn't believe what she was hearing. For Mercari, it's surreal seeing that horrible place on the news.

Exhausted from the hospital trips, police interviews, and emotional effects of their adventure, Jasmine can do little more than give a small smile to her family, beckoning them to sit with her.

"Take a seat by your mom," says Kel. They settle on the couch. "Listen," he says, his arms around Jasmine as Mercari settles next to her mother. "What I did to you was totally wrong. I walked out on you two without explanation. I felt like... our marriage was falling apart, and nobody wanted me here. But that's no excuse. Instead of making it right, I disappeared."

"I'm sorry, Kel. I'm to blame for this," says Jasmine, leaning into his chest, her other arm around Mercari, holding her close.

"I messed up. Maybe we both did. But I want to make it right," says Kel. "I… just want my family back." His voice tears up.

"I love you so much, Dad," says Mercari, taking his hand. "You saved me. Both of you did. I'll never forget it." She hugs him tight, and they hold each other, a family reunited.

The End